Total-E-Bound Publishing books by Elizabeth Lapthorne:

The Agency Volume One
Flirting With Danger
Courting Passion

Wicked Teacher

I0542045

THE AGENCY
Volume Two

Passionate Immunity

Passionate Vengeance

ELIZABETH
LAPTHORNE

The Agency Volume Two
ISBN # 978-1-78184-593-6
©Copyright Elizabeth Lapthorne 2013
Cover Art by Posh Gosh ©Copyright 2013
Interior text design by Claire Siemaszkiewicz
Total-E-Bound Publishing

Published in 2013 by Total-E-Bound Publishing, Think Tank, Ruston Way, Lincoln, LN6 7FL, United Kingdom.

Total-E-Bound Publishing is an imprint of Total-E-Ntwined Limited.

.

PASSIONATE IMMUNITY

Prologue

"... No, I know I can disarm this," Taylor insisted as George leaned over her shoulder, his breath warm and sensual on the nape of her neck.

"We won't have enough time, love. I think we should take our window here and run. Otherwise we'll never make it."

Taylor's heart pounded, and not merely from the fear of their imminent death. A bead of sweat ran down the curve of her spine. Her pussy throbbed hungrily. Every inch of her skin tingled with the certain, deeply sexual knowledge that this man was her soul mate. She could feel the spark of electric awareness between them as his body pressed against hers. She'd been branded by him, and she wasn't sure he even knew it.

In that heartbeat of time nothing else mattered. Not the devastating bomb she struggled to defuse, not the fact it went against every rule in the book – and a few others beside that – for them to be together. She loved this man heart, body and soul. The heat she read in George's wild eyes proved he felt the same.

"We might make it," she whispered, her meaning relating to the bomb as well as the serious turn to their initially light-hearted affair.

One more heartbeat lengthened between them as her mind flashed over every erotic, breathless moment they'd shared together. She could envision them so clearly, wrapped around each other's body, offering everything, baring their very souls to one another that her breath froze in her lungs.

George nodded.

"We'll make it," he repeated with conviction. "Do your thing, love, I'm right here beside you."

Heat flooded her body again as George wrapped an arm around her shoulder, drawing his chest flush against her side. She bent back to the task of saving the world – but just as importantly, saving the two of them so they could once again burn the sheets up together. In a single glance she assessed the bomb and knew exactly which wire to cut.

Turning her head, Taylor caught George's gaze with her own piercing blue eyes.

"Shall we go for the money shot?" she teased.

Her heart pounded, her body sang with adrenaline as she flew high on the excitement of the moment. This was far from her first time cheating death and she knew one day Death would beat her out and that would be it. Today would not be that day.

George understood her excitement as few others could ever hope to. He grinned sexily at her, setting her clit and nipples to tingling unbearably. She wanted nothing more than to pounce on him, rip their clothes off and sink herself onto his thick, hard cock.

"Every shot is a money shot with you, darling," George purred.

Taylor felt herself melt, her body humming for her lover in a desperate craving that never went away, no matter how frequently they satisfied their urges.

She reached her hand forward, the clippers held steadily as she placed them either side of the white wire and –

The sound of footsteps echoed down the deserted hallway. It took Kimberly Melmoth a couple of seconds to realise why this noise had dragged her reluctantly from her erotic thriller. Time had seeped away during her 'short mental break' from the laboratory work she was supposed to be fully focused on.

Her tiny cubicle had been transformed in her mind to a dark corridor. She could almost feel George's hard body pressed to hers and a large, complex bomb needing to be defused. Glancing at the clock at the bottom corner of her computer, she noticed with a twinge of guilt that almost half an hour had passed since she'd last checked.

The footsteps echoed. Apparently the laboratory had emptied while she'd been lost in the fictional world. Everyone had left for the evening. Her subconscious understood her vulnerability in being alone and had roused her from the addictive story. With her life going nowhere fast, books — erotic or otherwise — had become a solace. They allowed Kimber to lose herself in excitement and adventure, to passionately explore all manner of things she longed for.

Currently, her real life lacked anything not related to her work and…well…more work.

Kimber stuffed the paperback in her handbag and snapped her bottom desk drawer closed. Her heart raced as the footsteps paused outside the door to her shared office. People didn't just drop by here. Not only was the lab protected by a security system, to anyone not used to the layout it was a labyrinth. Her 'office' — the tiny shared space with three desks crammed side by side, with hardly enough room to push one's chair back without hitting the wall, could hardly be called such a thing — was squashed in what used to be a side corridor joining two separate areas of the laboratories. It was not a simple or logical place to find anyone.

Kimber wondered if a visitor from earlier in the afternoon might have got lost and been attracted by the lights in her work area. She had only just placed her hand on the computer's mouse to check her calendar and see if there'd been any dignitaries visiting when she felt the presence of the other person enter the open doorway.

Feeling equal parts flustered and caught out—a quick glance assured her the book was still packed away—she looked up. The man who filled the doorway was the large, dark-skinned form of her friend's husband.

"Preston!" Kimber ran a hand through her hair. Usually she kept her shoulder-length, straw-blonde curls firmly restrained either in a ponytail or French braid, but she had taken it out due to a headache earlier.

Feeling somewhat conscious of the mess she must look, she retrieved an elastic band from around her wrist and pulled her hair back as she stood.

"Kimberly," Preston greeted her warmly. "It's been too long. Felicity keeps swearing to invite you over for tea, but you know how it is. She's been involved in one convoluted project after another lately."

Kimber opened her arms to hug the tall man. Surprise had her nodding, struggling for words. She looked around, expecting to see Felicity entering the tiny office behind Preston.

Confused when Felicity was nowhere to be seen, but not overly upset, Kimber pulled a chair out from a neighbouring cubicle.

"Please, sit. Can I get you some truly terrible coffee? Or some tea—I have bags in my desk drawer," she offered.

Preston sat. "No, but thank you."

She scooted her chair back so their legs wouldn't bump, then sat.

"You don't look upset," Kimber continued, still trying to puzzle out Preston's unexpected arrival. "I'm assuming everything is okay with Felicity and the girls? So to what do I owe this pleasure? I'm surprised to find you down here."

Felicity Jones had been one of the resident tutors at Kimber's university. The women had formed a close friendship during her final-year Biochemistry project. Although Kimber's passions lay more in the virology field, she'd remained pragmatic. Jobs were scarce in that area and she had bills and a mortgage to pay. Kimber kept abreast of the recent developments in the field of biology, but had been grateful to not be one of the many newly-minted scientists who struggled to find work.

Preston had always kept quiet on what his job for the government entailed exactly, but Felicity had let enough hints drop that Kimber knew it was almost certainly even more adventurous than her daydreams could believe.

"I can't go into too much detail," Preston said as he rested his elbows on his thighs. "But in the course of an investigation I've come across some activity that needs further research. My main problem is it's in the medical field—vaccine work. Immune responses and engineering diseases from what I can gather. As I'm sure you can believe, that is far outside the scope of my knowledge, especially as even the rudimentary data I've collected so far is well beyond my basic understanding. It's complex and I'm totally out of my depth."

As Preston spoke Kimber picked up a pen and pulled a notebook closer to hand. Old habits died hard and she had long ago learnt to take notes when someone gave her information. The general terms he used to explain, however, stopped her from writing anything just yet.

"What kind of information do you need from me?" she asked, intrigued.

"I'm not certain yet," Preston replied. He sounded frustrated. A frown twisted his dark features and creases appeared between his eyes.

She could tell his annoyance wasn't directed at her, personally.

"I need you to come work for me for a short period. Maybe just a few days, but possibly as much as a week."

Kimber felt her eyes widen in surprise. Her mind raced.

"I have plenty of leave," she replied. "Heaven knows it's been forever since I've been on holiday. But Preston…I still don't really understand. Surely you have people and resources at your work already who have far more knowledge than I do. Why me?"

Preston winced and looked around her tiny, empty office. He pushed his chair forward and lowered his voice.

Excitement thrummed through her veins as she bent her head to listen more closely.

"I'm not sharing state secrets," he assured her, "but I know you well enough to believe you can keep this to yourself, Kimber."

Kimberly nodded, moving forward on her chair, eager to hear more. Preston took a careful breath and studied her. She could see him weighing his options.

"I'm cleaning up a mess left by a traitor. The woman who held my job before me betrayed this country and the Agency I work for. There's been an audit of her files and documents. It's been brought to my attention there might be something underhand occurring in a medical clinic we sometimes use as a front. The finance people don't fully understand the medical jargon, but because this woman betrayed us, many of the upper managers are feeling understandably paranoid. You're not involved with any of this history or the politics intertwined with this, so to a degree that makes you completely trustworthy. Better still, I can personally vouch for you and your integrity."

Kimber smiled. The praise from Preston made her feel warm. Feeling grateful and a bit shy, she tugged on a lock of her hair. Preston continued.

"I plan to assign two of my best agents to work with you. A seasoned veteran and his new partner, a younger but still excellent man. They'll be there to protect you, but also do all the wet work. Felicity will have my balls if any harm comes to you, so you're to gather intelligence, go through the files and possibly help scout out the facility. No heroics and no danger. I can already see the stars in your eyes, but I'm telling you it will mostly be paperwork. Going over reports and the like. I'd think that would be all the adventure you come across and then my men will take over. Are we clear?"

Kimber's eyes widened once again as Preston's meaning sank in. It might be only the one job, but she was going to assist in a real, honest-to-goodness *investigation*.

"I get to go on a mission?" she repeated, all his cautions, warnings and strict rules ignored as her imagination took wild flight. "I'd get to be...what? A secret agent? Working for Queen and country? I'd be a female James Bond? Truly?"

"Not in the least. Kimberly Melmoth, you listen to me," Preston insisted, strain lines already showing around the corner of his mouth. Were it not physically impossible, Kimber could well believe he'd have gone several shades paler.

"Kimber, this will be paperwork, data-mining reports and possibly a simple, placid look through a medical facility. No more. Do you hear me?"

She outwardly assented. Had she been entirely truthful about the matter—and not caught up in a dozen flights of fancy—she would have had to admit Preston's strictures had gone in one ear and straight out the other. She beamed as if he had given her the moon. With a head full of every adventure novel and action movie she had ever seen racing behind her eyes she imagined shootouts, thrilling car chases and desperate heroes racing through flames as buildings exploded around them.

Kimber saw herself in a slinky cocktail dress with impossibly high stiletto heels. In her fantasy she was running out of an architecturally gorgeous building. The hero would sweep her into his arms after they'd defied death yet again. He would passionately kiss her, his lips pressed to hers as she wound her legs around his waist, and his long brown hair would sweep over her face, shielding her from any onlookers. Then her hero would lift her up into his strong arms and carry her off—

"Holy fuck, what have I done?" Preston muttered. It took Kimber a moment to register his words, her mind consumed by her daydream.

She blinked and looked at him, attempting to appear innocent. "What? What?"

Preston rubbed a hand over his face and mumbled something to himself.

Cocking her head to the side, Kimber leaned in and caught the tail end of it.

"...thank fuck Walters at least has a solid head on his shoulders. Flick is going to murder me when I tell her what I've set in motion."

"Why will Felicity kill you? You said it yourself, I'll be fine. Though it won't be my fault if while I'm at the medical facility I happen to snoop a little and—"

"Not a chance in hell," Preston snapped. Kimber deflated. For the first time ever she saw the determined, powerful man he could be in his professional life.

"But—"

"No. End of story. If you go off half-cocked, Kimberly, I won't bring you in at all."

Kimber swallowed hard, feeling chastised. She nodded meekly. Now she'd had the lure of adventure, passion and romance dangled in front of her she refused to have it taken away again. Preston wouldn't be there when it counted, only two of his underlings. She could easily bend the rules once she was out from under his scrutiny.

Wanting to change the subject before Preston retracted his offer, she asked the next thing that entered her head, hoping to defuse the situation.

"Who's Walters? You mentioned him just a minute ago."

"Tristan Walters is one of our most seasoned agents," Preston replied, seemingly distracted. "He lost his partner just a few months ago and is currently helping to give a bit of polish to one of our newer recruits, Lucas Sloan. They're the men I plan to assign to this case. Once you've given them a good understanding of what's going on it will be they—and not you—who put this all to bed. So please don't get any wild ideas."

Kimber stood, smart enough to not reply one way or the other to that comment. She shrugged out of her white lab coat and gathered her belongings. She still needed to clean up her samples and get herself organised for the following morning. While it was still fresh in her mind, she scribbled out a quick list of tasks she needed to do in her notebook. After a minute there were a dozen or more items she needed to perform to wrap up her current workload and take leave without anything falling behind.

"Do I start tomorrow?" she asked.

Preston nodded.

"Give me time to bring Walters and Sloan up to date," he said. Preston drew out a business card from the inner pocket of his jacket. "Will eleven tomorrow morning be too early for you to have this all sorted out?"

Kimber shook her head. "Oh no, I usually start early. I can email my manager and request the leave before I go home tonight. I'll just need to talk to my co-workers and make sure a few of my longer-term tests can be covered, but it won't be a hassle. Heaven knows I've helped everyone else often enough."

Preston stood and faced her, looking faintly pained. Kimber laughed and hugged her friend once more.

"I'm not some dewy-eyed ingénue, Preston," she insisted. "You've already assigned what I can only presume will be two hulking, large bodyguards for a simple reconnaissance mission. What could possibly go wrong with reading a bunch of reports and nosing around a medical lab?"

Preston winced and tugged her ponytail in a brotherly fashion.

"Never say that, Kimber. Never say 'what could possibly go wrong'. All too often it's the unknown factors that trip you up. If I genuinely thought there was the least bit of danger I'd have never mentioned it, I'd forbid you to come anywhere near this. But Felicity has told me so often how much you long for adventure, and how a simple case like this would be perfect for you. I thought it would be fun. I didn't realise I'd start getting ulcer pains before I'd even left from offering this to you."

Kimber grinned. "Don't worry, Preston. You and Felicity are wonderful friends, and I appreciate this. You said so yourself, there's nothing to be concerned about, this will be a simple matter of explaining some research and reports. There's no need for you to work yourself up over it. I can handle myself. Besides, I bet this will be fun."

"That's what I'm afraid of," Preston replied glumly.

Kimber grinned once more as her friend turned and walked out of her office like a man heading towards his doom.

Chapter One

Tristan Walters winced as he rotated his right shoulder. It was more from the memory of the pain he'd been in for almost two months, rather than the actual stiffness he felt now. The gunshot wound, still fresh in his mind, had healed as much as it ever would. Only the week before he had been confident the worst of his discomfort was behind him.

But now, with London expecting some bad weather, his shoulder ached once more.

"I think I can safely forecast rain in the next few hours," he told the young, blond man sitting at the desk opposite him. Tristan ran his left hand over his dark brown hair, conscious even without a mirror of the silver beginning to salt itself through the strands.

It hadn't been until two months ago he'd started to feel his age. He'd lost his Agency partner in the same fight he'd sustained the gunshot wound. Jasper Peterson and he had worked together for almost ten years. Neither of them had been virginal novices—

they both had known full well the danger and risk inherent in their work.

That knowledge hadn't stopped the pain of mourning a good friend and colleague. Preston Jones had transferred in while Tristan had still been doped up on a remarkable cocktail of painkillers and slowly recovering in the hospital. Preston had taken over from their old manager—who had been in collusion with the terrorist directly responsible for Jasper's death.

When Tristan had returned to work less than a fortnight later, Preston had brought in Lucas Sloan and introduced him to Tristan as his new partner. Like many partnerships, they had begun rockily. Tristan hadn't been in the mood to break in a newbie, especially not one who appeared to have only just passed his thirtieth birthday. The man had been still wet behind his ears and that was something Tristan wasn't sure he'd wanted to be responsible for.

Feeling like the stereotypical cranky old man despite the fact he still had a few months before he hit forty, Tristan hadn't exactly given the man a warm welcome.

Keeping his temper on a short fuse was the fact he'd been relegated to desk duty—mostly paperwork and organising the schedules and week's roster. It was all busy stuff designed to keep up the appearance of him being one of the team. Tristan found himself frequently grinding his teeth in order to stop himself from snapping at his colleagues. Being chained to his desk felt like the end of the world, and despite knowing it was temporary, the mind-numbing nature of the files was soul-destroying.

All through this Lucas had been patient, something Tristan had appreciated but had not been able to bring himself to acknowledge. As he'd healed, Tristan had found himself chuckling now and then at a quip Lucas would make, or zinging the man with a witty rejoinder.

It had been almost a fortnight after their introduction when Tristan had first invited Lucas down to the local for a pint after their day had ended. The two men had started talking superficially, but the wind-down sessions after a shift had become a semi-regular thing. Slowly, the ice had begun to melt between them.

Now, two months later, while Tristan didn't think they would qualify as best mates, there was a level of understanding and trust between them. Time and experience would solidify their partnership.

"Who needs the weatherman when my partner is a walking meteorology indicator?" Lucas joked. He tilted his head, the long strands of his blond fringe fell into his eyes and Tristan snorted.

"Bet you twenty pounds over the next six months my shoulder and I predict the rain more accurately than the Met Office do, too."

Lucas appeared to be about to reply when Preston stuck his head out of the door to his office. "Walters! Sloan! In here, now."

The two men exchanged equally blank looks.

"Do you know what this is about?" Lucas asked. They both pushed away from their desks and stood.

"Not a clue," Tristan replied. "I was about to ask you the same thing. I have my final medical later this afternoon to clear me for active duty. We weren't supposed to be assigned anything new until tomorrow."

"Then it must be something big," Lucas postulated as they walked side by side towards Preston's office.

"Or boring," Tristan added pessimistically.

Preston Jones had shown himself to be a tough but fair leader. His door always stood open unless he was in the middle of a private meeting. Over six foot of muscle, still evidently in shape from his years in the Army and with a no-nonsense manner, Preston had gone over well with most of the agents. His black hair was still buzzed short, but there was no mistaking the sharp look in his dark eyes. Unlike his field days though, Preston now generally wore dark suits and looked the part of a manager.

Tristan and Lucas both deeply respected the man.

Preston stood behind his desk with a manila folder in one hand and a sheaf of papers in the other. He glanced up as Lucas and Tristan entered the office. Preston nodded to the two chairs in front of his desk and returned his attention to the reports he seemed to be in the middle of sorting.

"Close the door and have a seat, gentlemen," Preston said without looking at either of them again.

Tristan held out a hand and slowly pushed the door closed. Simultaneously both he and Lucas exchanged another silent glance. Tristan cocked an eyebrow. Lucas shrugged.

The partners sat in unison, a clear show of mutual support and solidarity that reminded Tristan how far they'd come in recent months.

"Neither of you are in the shit," Preston assured them. He met both of their gazes in turn for a brief moment before piling the papers and folder on the top of his desk.

"I've checked with Morrison down in the medical wing. He assures me that as long as you take it easy you'll be right for active duty as of this evening," Preston continued as he took his seat. "Sorting out the mess left by my predecessor is taking longer than anyone had guessed. Most of her cases have been cleared as untainted, but there's one in particular that has captured the auditor's attention."

The room filled with an uneasy tension. Emma Henley had been a well-liked, respected team leader within the Agency. Discovering her knowingly and actively working against their objectives to keep their country safe had been a blow to many. Making the matter even more personal, if possible, it had been her actions that had led to Jasper Peterson being murdered. The loss and Henley's betrayal were still raw with Tristan.

"What do you need?" Tristan asked, moving forward in his chair, eager for anything he could do to help reverse the damage one woman had created.

Lucas leaned closer to Preston's desk. Without words Tristan could see his new partner fully understood the importance of doing something to avenge Jasper.

Preston's mouth twisted into a faint smile.

"Morrison said you'd need to take it easy, so this won't be an all-guns-blazing mission. Indeed, for now at least it will hopefully remain largely a data-mining and paperwork-based task," he chided.

"Henley appears to have worked for over a year on something she's labelled as Project Immunity," Preston said. "From what I can gather there's a medical facility that the Agency has used numerous times as a cover. As far as that goes it's nothing unusual. What grabbed the auditor's notice, however, was after a cursory inspection of their paperwork they discovered the facility is doing research Henley appeared to be sponsoring through back channels. I don't understand exactly how they've connected it, but the financial auditors assure me there's a twisted, convoluted path between discretionary funds connected with us and this facility."

"If the medical practice lets us use them for cover from time to time then isn't it to be expected there'd be a link between us and payment for them?" Lucas asked, clearly puzzled.

Preston shook his head.

"If the funds are for discreet cover stories then the sources should correlate with those jobs. This is something separate," he pointed out. "More importantly these all seem to tie back in with a single project. Also, Immunity doesn't link back in anywhere else the auditors can find. It almost appears to be an off-the-books project Henley headed up. Which was exactly the kind of shady dealings they wanted to uncover. Project Immunity is a big question mark right now and Finance has done what they can. They're not able to satisfactorily put upper management's fears to rest so it's been handballed over to us."

"So you want us to go out there and check the place out?" Tristan asked.

Until this moment Tristan hadn't fully appreciated just how much he had missed his work. His heart had sped up at the thought of a new mission, especially one to help close the case on Emma Henley. He had begun to take his job for granted. While he'd been sidelined it had been easy to focus on getting better, taking things step by step. Now, however, he felt eager to get back into the swing of his regular life.

"If we leave in the next twenty minutes we can be ahead of the peak-hour commuter traffic," Lucas added with a quick glance at his watch. "I'll go grab keys to one of the pool cars and—"

"I'm not sure which part of 'paperwork-based' you lads misunderstood," Preston cut in mildly, "but last time I checked my dictionary it means sitting on your asses and going through files, such as these ones here on my desk. As I said, I want no blazing guns, no heroics and definitely no bloodshed. I want this to be strictly by the book, at least until all hell breaks loose. That means the two of you will be going over the paperwork with a fine–toothed comb."

He waved a dark hand at the mound of papers littering his desk. Simultaneously both men sat back in their chairs. Tristan cast a dismal look at the piles of paper then shared a grimace with Lucas but neither man said a word of protest.

He'd not admit it aloud, but Tristan knew Jones could easily have picked any number of other agents equally desperate as he to right the wrongs Emma Henley had done to their Agency. Tristan wasn't the only agent who had lost his partner, and he was far from the only person present on shift today who would work his fingers to the bone to receive closure and atone for the dark smear on their reputation.

Preston was giving him a gift. He wouldn't do anything to make his superior regret handing this to him. Lucas appeared less than thrilled with the concept of many hours' worth of sifting through paperwork, but his partner thankfully remained silent. Tristan was grateful Lucas wouldn't utter a word in protest.

"I realise much of the scientific research in here will be over both your heads," Preston continued when it was clear neither agent would dissent to their task. "I've already tapped a lady I know to assist in that side of the mission. She isn't Agency, but I have given her temporary epsilon-level clearance. That should be enough for her to sort through the files, discuss anything she needs with you both and make her report without compromising any overly sensitive data."

"You've brought someone external into this?" Tristan repeated. He exchanged a glance with his partner. "Surely one of the medical staff—"

"My superiors want this handled quickly and quietly," Preston insisted. "Taking out one of our own staff away from their regular duties isn't the best option here. Besides, a fresh set of eyes is what we need. She won't arrive with preconceived notions and that gives us an edge. Henceforth, until you submit your final reports, this is your only priority. You'll discover as you sort through this it appears as if human experimentation has been involved in the project. I'm sure I don't have to begin to explain what a disaster this might prove to be."

"All the more reason to keep this in-house," Lucas supported Tristan's concerns. "Bringing a civilian into this could make matters worse. What if she wants to report what we discover to some medical board or other authority? We can't control her. As a result we won't be fully in control of the investigation, either."

"This woman has been a friend of my wife's for almost ten years," Preston said. "Felicity adores her. I know Kimberly almost as well as I know my own children. I hope you can both take my word that she is an honourable woman and someone you can trust to advise you in this. You'll both work with Kimber, gentlemen, and treat her as an equal, as if she were simply another member of this Agency. More importantly, unless you want to face my wife's formidable wrath, should anything even give off the faintest whiff of danger, you are to protect Kimber and retreat immediately. I'll have no compunction whatsoever in feeding you both to Felicity should something go astray. Have I made myself clear?"

"Yes, sir," both men responded automatically.

Jones collected the piles of reports and folders from his desk. Tristan and Lucas stood and reached over to each take some as Preston held them out.

"I'll bring Kimber over to the Conference room when she arrives," Preston concluded their meeting. "It shouldn't be too long. In the meanwhile, it might help if you both started to sort through all this mess. These files are restricted to Code Orange, so I hope neither of you have any long weekends away planned."

Tristan and Lucas both gathered the rest of the papers. Code Orange meant they couldn't remove any of the documents from the Agency's main office area, and any personal notes they took had to be encrypted enough so random strangers couldn't make sense of the data. Over the years Tristan had become so used to these measures he often wrote half of his shopping list in his private coding system before he even realised it.

Following Lucas out of Preston's office, Tristan let his mind wander over their new mission. A slight ache in his shoulder from carrying the mountain of paperwork along with the incoming storm reminded him he was no longer young. But he couldn't help the thrill of a new case, a new puzzle and a fresh start that zinged through his body. He was as addicted as any junkie to this work, and in his heart he knew they'd have to bury him before he quit.

The high of saving the world, setting wrongs right and protecting his country had settled deeply into his blood and bones. He might not be a spring chicken like Lucas, but it was a long time before he'd be old, too. The tiniest smatterings of silver meant nothing. He had age, experience and knowledge. A bullet in his shoulder couldn't take that from him, nor could a traitorous bitch like Emma Henley.

Feeling rejuvenated, Tristan dumped the papers onto the conference table and took a seat opposite Lucas. The blond looked overwhelmed.

"Where the hell do we start?" he moaned. Tristan chuckled and picked up the nearest manila folder.

"At the start, my boy," Tristan replied. "Let's get these folders in chronological order and work from there. If we both scan the files we can brainstorm from there."

Sighing, Lucas agreed and the two men set to work.

* * * *

"Here's another case file," Lucas said distractedly. "Jeremy Bowman. Male, Caucasian, age twenty-seven."

"Add him to the pile," Tristan replied with a sinking sensation in his stomach. Hell. That made four references to individuals and they were barely halfway through the reams of paper. He ran a hand through his hair.

"Is there more data this time?" he asked Lucas, hope flickering in his gut. The small flame spluttered as Lucas shook his head.

"No, man, just an admittance form and half-page of indecipherable scrawl like the others."

"Damn it. There must be more data somewhere," Tristan muttered. "My instinct is screaming at me. These four patients are pivotal somehow. We just need to put them in the right part of the puzzle."

"Heads up," Lucas replied. "Incoming, mate."

His mind still submerged in the mental puzzle before him, Tristan lifted his eyes to glance out of the wall of windows from the Conference Room into the office at large. It took him half a minute to compute what his gaze showed him. By the time he realised Preston was leading his 'Civilian Consultant' their way the large, dark man had already opened the door for the petite, curvy blonde woman. A head full of spiralling curls bounced as she walked, eagerness sparkling from her like an electric current.

Her grin was so wide Tristan felt surprised it didn't have the power to light up the entire city block.

"Gentlemen," Preston boomed in his deep voice. He halted in the threshold.

Both Tristan and Lucas stood politely.

"This is Kimberly Melmoth, the scientist I informed you of earlier this morning. She will be assisting you in going over these papers. Kimber, this is Lucas Sloan and Tristan Walters. Please listen to them. They'll stop you doing anything…impulsive."

Tristan couldn't swear to it later, but he thought he heard ever so faintly under Preston's breath a murmured "I hope" after his last word.

Kimberly had reached out to shake Lucas' hand while Preston had introduced them. Then she turned her full focus onto Tristan, smiled blindingly at him and reached out her hand. Unable to help himself, he found an answering smile crease his face. Leaning forward he reached out and clasped Kimber's palm in his. Tristan wrapped his fingers around her skin, conscious of her long, slender digits feeling warm against him.

Heat—potent and fierce—gripped his body. Kimberly's eyes were a warm, bright shade of blue reminiscent of a Fiji lagoon. Energy hummed beneath her skin, an excitement so visceral she practically vibrated with it. The woman clearly felt thrilled to be a part of this mission. Her pale skin was delicately flushed, whether from her enjoyment of her new job or their contact he had no clue.

"I'm so pleased to meet you," she spoke, her voice breathless. Their gaze held a moment longer than was usual, both of them seemingly unable to break the contact. Tristan had never felt such an instant snap of connection to anyone before. The chemistry was immediate and intense.

For the first time Tristan felt at a loss for words. Preston's tone broke through the haze.

"As I've already explained at length to Kimber, this is predominantly a paper- and report-based job. At this stage there is no need for any of you to leave this room, let alone go out there searching for trouble."

"We'll keep her safe," Tristan replied. He reluctantly let go of her soft hand. The flush over Kimber's cheeks became noticeably darker.

"I'm not some four-year-old needing to hold hands before I cross the road," she insisted. The glare she gave Preston indicated to Tristan this was not the first time she'd tried to persuade the man of her capabilities. She appeared so small, delicate even. A hot, exceedingly masculine part of Tristan wondered what the fuck Preston was doing letting such an intriguing, passionate woman enter into this life.

As Tristan had so recently been reminded of with the death of Jasper, this wasn't some game for kids or innocents. It was the harsh, cruel realities of the worst side of life. Preston had mentioned this woman was a close friend of his wife's. What was the man thinking?

He was tempted to give his boss a cutting piece of his mind. Lucas appeared to sense the change in undertone of the room and interjected before Tristan could get himself fired for insubordination.

"Actually it's a good thing you're here, Ms Melmoth." Lucas beamed a warm smile at the woman.

A spike of jealousy seared through Tristan, taking him brutally by surprise. What the fuck? He'd barely met the woman and already he felt possessive? Was he losing his mind?

"We've found these references to 'subjects', but haven't been able to ascertain exactly what they mean. Perhaps if you could have a look…"

Kimber reached out to take the thin file Lucas handed her and focused her attention on the two sheets of paper held within the manila folder. Preston glanced at them each in turn. Seeming satisfied, he left the room and closed the door behind him.

"Where's the rest of it?" Kimberly asked, glancing first at Lucas, then turned her head to capture Tristan's gaze with her own.

For the second time in as many minutes Tristan felt his brain fry. Forcing himself to stick to the subject at hand, he cleared his throat and answered before Lucas could. "We're only part way through," he explained. "The records are a mess, presumably any number of agents have gone over them. Lucas and I were in the process of chronologically ordering everything as best we could. So far we haven't found more than those two sheets for any of the subjects mentioned."

"Subjects," she repeated with an emphasis on the 's'. "How many have you found?"

"Four so far," Tristan replied.

Understanding dawned across Lucas' face. His partner cast him a knowing smile, sat back and began to once again go through the paperwork. Tristan easily shrugged his partner's humour off.

Kimber appeared unaware of the silent exchange between the two men.

"Well, I guess I should start reading and catching up," she said. Her light tone and happy smile clearly conveyed her excitement. Tristan shook his head. Her pleasure at such a simple, usually mundane task was contagious.

"Are you always so thrilled by paperwork?" he asked.

Her answering grin was enormous. "I've read more spy thrillers than I care to think about," she replied. "I know Preston insists this will be boring, mundane and totally anti-climactic. But something deep inside me insists this is my big adventure. I've craved excitement and action since I was a little girl running around playing thieves and coppers. I can't explain why I know this will be huge for me, but I just do. I'm thrilled to be here."

Lucas and Tristan exchanged a look. Despite the fact Tristan had her pegged somewhere in her mid-thirties, right now Kimber could pass for an eager schoolgirl about to go out on her first real date. She all but hummed with vibrant anticipation.

"I hope you're as thrilled after you've spent two or three hours on these uncomfortable seats, reading through mounds of this paperwork," Tristan finally replied, unwilling and unable to squash her pleasure.

Kimber met his gaze, her blue eyes sparkling.

"In such company, I'm sure I'll be just as exhilarated," she said.

Heat seared through Tristan, his cock hardened at the sensuality in her words.

Did she just…? His brain registered the dual meaning of her words. Part of him refuted the hidden meaning she alluded to, while the naughty smile and wicked glint in her eyes assured him that yes, she had meant for her words to hint at what he'd thought.

Saucy wench!

Tristan grinned more slowly this time, the taunting smile melting over his face as his blood thickened with wicked lust.

"Well then," he purred. The day suddenly had an unexpected depth to it. "Never let it be said I wasn't accommodating to a lady's desires. Where would you like to start?"

Kimber's gaze turned sexy.

Tristan couldn't wait for this sensual game of back-and-forth to unfold.

Chapter Two

Kimber had craved adventure and passion for so long. Now that she was here she could hardly believe it. Ten minutes after sitting down she still felt the electric hum of excitement racing through her body, keeping her faintly on edge and jittery. Having Tristan seated next to her in no way helped calm the thrills arcing through her system. The man was living and breathing *sex*. She felt overly aware of the fact that her skin prickled with sensual awareness of him.

How any female could do the least bit of work around this man eluded her. His body was strong and lean—an athlete's form full of sleek muscles. Kimber found the mixture of strength and agility he showed in his every move intoxicating.

Warm eyes crinkled around the edges with barely suppressed laughter, his amusement clear. Dark brown hair had been mussed by, she suspected, too many finger-combings, showing the faintest hint of silver at the edges. Kimber hazarded a guess that

Tristan was very close to forty, perhaps just scraping past the important milestone by no more than a year.

Even more attractive to her was his calm demeanour and take-charge attitude. As a scientist she found all too often men became uncomfortable and even put off by the fact she had a solid, working knowledge of many convoluted processes. It became frustrating after a while, especially when work was the furthest thing from her mind.

While Tristan had barely said more than a dozen words in the time they had been studying the plethora of documents, Kimber had enjoyed his quiet, masculine assurance. He appeared neither impressed nor cowed by the fact she had a brain and understanding beyond his ken.

This pleasure, mingled with her fierce physical reaction to him, heightened her anticipation of what lay before them, both with their adventure and their sexual potency. Arousal made her mind sharp, and her heart pound furiously.

Despite the mammoth drain on her attention, Kimber somehow managed to force herself to pay attention to the documents she surveyed.

"Much of this appears to be background research," she finally spoke after nearly a quarter of an hour studying the various piles Lucas and Tristan had been sorting. "I've found photocopies from various medical texts, journal articles, magazines and the like. It's a real mishmash of sources all somehow connected to the immune system and different research projects that are both ongoing and recently presented."

"Can you give us the short and sweet version?" Lucas asked, a hopeful lilt in his voice.

Kimber chuckled, enjoying his enthusiasm. "If it's needed I can explain as much or as little as you both require. Right now I'm trying to make sense of how this all pieces together." Kimber frowned as she moved the papers into different piles while speaking her thoughts aloud. "All this seems to be general background like I mentioned," she said slowly, trying to put it together in her mind. "Other than the fact it's all related to the immune system, healing, white blood cells, that overall area, it doesn't seem specific in any other way."

The silence in the conference room felt weighted for a moment. The prickling sensation that she was missing something had Kimber looking up, glancing between the two men. They watched each other, appearing to almost communicate without words.

"What?" she interjected, feeling as if she had interrupted them despite the fact that they remained silent.

It was Lucas who replied after another long moment. "This was Henley's project, Preston's predecessor. From what I've heard she was a regular manager and agent, no special interest in science. It makes sense she'd need background information if she was focused on a medical project like this."

"Okay." Kimber nodded. "These are what I find really interesting though," she continued, picking up nine slim folders. "There are nine folders here, seeming to represent nine individuals. Eight appear to have died if the big, red 'Closed' stamp is anything to judge by, but the final one is still open."

"We've already checked those." Tristan frowned as he spoke. "We couldn't understand their importance."

"That's because my money would be on your old manager, this Henley woman, having copied these without permission," Kimber replied. "Medical records are sacrosanct. I can guarantee she wasn't supposed to have these. There's so little information here I can't understand why she'd have risked everything to take these two sheets."

"There's plenty of data," Lucas protested. "Their application form has next-of-kin contacts, all their physical details, personal information. It's an identity thief's wet dream."

"I think that's why she photocopied these pages," Kimber agreed. "To keep a record or maybe do a search on these people. It's this second sheet that really intrigues me."

Kimber spread out the nine files. She opened the folders and collated the second, briefer sheet from four of them to show how similar they all were.

"I still can't read it, this is incomplete," she explained almost apologetically, "but I understand enough for us to get a start on it. This number here, one-twenty over ninety, is the subject's blood pressure. And here, I'm confident this is their temperature and weight, their reflective reactions and so forth."

"So these files are just annual check-ups?" Lucas said, clearly dismayed.

Kimber shook her head.

"No. I think they're baseline physical statistics," she said. The moment the words were out of her mouth she hoped she wasn't making a fool of herself and jumping the gun. She pointed to the last few lines midway down the sheet of paper.

"See, they're all dated. And this is the amount each individual was injected with, calculated from their age, race and weight. In any experiment you need the control levels, the baseline with which to compare whatever data you seek to interpret. I think Henley copied these files at the start of the experiment to have the personal data of each test subject and unwittingly copied this sheet too."

"You really think this was some sort of experiment?" Tristan repeated.

Kimber searched his face, worried. He appeared thoughtful, reflective. He didn't look sceptical or disbelieving, but she could tell he wasn't sold on her idea.

"Without the rest of the files I can't be certain of anything," she admitted. "I need to see the full data, even if it's cryptic or in some form of shorthand I should be able to get a far better idea."

"We can get you copies," Lucas agreed.

Kimber shook her head.

"It would be better if I go to the facility and look for myself," she insisted. "Copies could prove bothersome in a legal sense. The Agency currently can deny knowledge of this invasion of privacy. If you wilfully and knowingly copy these medical records it could prove sticky in court. All I'd need would be a few minutes to sort out what's happening. From there Preston or his managers can make the call."

Tristan shot her a hard look.

"This isn't a game," he said firmly. "You've got stars in your eyes, and believe me, it suits you. Regardless, there's not a chance in hell you're breaking into a medical facility with us."

"It can't possibly be that dangerous," she protested. No way did she want to be left behind. This was her chance for adventure, damn it. If Tristan thought she'd smile meekly and sit on the sidelines he was so wrong.

"Teenagers break and enter buildings every day," she said. "Junkies steal drugs, children sneak things into their pockets. The police almost never catch anyone who doesn't fall into their lap for these small offences. You're a professional. I bet you can have the three of us in and out of there in fifteen minutes before anyone even realises what we're doing."

"Preston would skin me alive," Tristan refused. "He's sworn to unleash his wife on us if we put you in the least danger."

Kimber snickered, unable to help the humour of the situation. "Felicity is barely five foot two," she replied with a laugh. "I bet she doesn't weigh fifty kilos soaking wet with her favourite knee-high leather boots on. A big, strong, manly man like yourself should not be terrified of such a small woman."

"Lady, I could probably lift you with just one arm," Tristan countered, not deterred in the least, "and your blinding determination to seek adventure and danger petrifies me. Any man who doesn't fear a headstrong woman even a little is a fool."

Kimber couldn't stop the grin spreading over her face. The more she bantered and spoke with Tristan, the more she liked him. He held a maturity and understanding most men she had met lacked. Better still, he easily held his own against her.

Not that she planned to let him win this particular struggle. It meant too much to her.

"With you there to protect me what could possibly go wrong?" she wheedled, her eyes innocently wide and her smile as charming as she could make it. "You can crack the lock, I can review the data and files super quickly and we can be back out in no time."

"Lucas and I can handle it," Tristan said. "We might let you wait in the car."

"We need Lucas to scout the exits, to…umm…" Kimber thought quickly, mentally reviewing the books and movies she had spent half a lifetime watching. "He'll need to guard our escape route, to check all is well outside and keep in touch with us inside. We need him to cover us."

A small quirk of Tristan's eyebrow showed Kimber he was struggling not to laugh. She didn't believe for a moment he wasn't taking this seriously, but it heartened her to see he could still understand the humour in their argument.

"Lucas and I are partners, a team. I'm not going to let him—"

"It's okay," Lucas interjected. Tristan shot him a hard, scowling look. The blond man winked cheekily at Kimber. She grinned in response, her spirits lifting.

"The more we argue about this, the bigger deal it will become to us," Lucas said. "If we just organise ourselves, get in and then out again, it shouldn't be a problem. Let her have some fun."

Tristan snorted and cast a disbelieving glance at his partner.

"So you're happy to take the heat from Preston if this all goes to hell then?"

Lucas beamed charmingly and shrugged.

"As she said, it's a simple thing. We've both done far more dangerous, complicated missions. It will be a snap."

"Neither of you would know a blood workup from a DNA profile from an electrophoresis gel analysis if it shook your hand and introduced itself to you," she concluded, trying for once to sound as snooty as possible. "Admit it, Walters, you need me there. Lucas can cover our arses and you can do all the dirty work. I'll do my best to sort out what's actually happening over there. Can we move on and brainstorm now, please?"

Tristan glanced from Lucas to her, then back to his partner again. Kimber could see the relaxing in his tense facial expression when he appeared to give in to the inevitable. Her heart skipped a beat at the thought of spending more time in an intimate surrounding with this delectable man. The conference room had little privacy with the floor to ceiling windows, anyone in the entire office area could look their way and see straight in. Privacy was not an option.

It didn't take a rocket scientist to understand that few things could draw two people together faster than highly charged situations such as one found on a mission. The thrill of breaking and entering a private property was a natural human emotion. Fear, heightened senses, sharpened wits and the resultant adrenaline was not just one of nature's best drugs, but a highly addictive aphrodisiac to boot.

Already they had enough sensual chemistry arcing between them to make her pussy slick with need. Kimber felt certain she would self-combust if she didn't feel her lips pressing hard against Tristan's soon. She longed to drink him down like a woman starved.

"Fine," Tristan capitulated with a tired sigh. Her attention reverted back to the situation at hand instantly as he took charge once again of their plans. "Lucas, make sure you've got at least three different escape routes plotted. One of them on foot for Kimber and I to run if we can't rendezvous at the designated point. If the police are called, likely there will be two groups on foot and a series of cars to block the main roads. We'll need the side streets and alleys as well as any underground access points we can use."

"I'll call the facility and find out their opening hours," Kimber said as she rummaged in her handbag for her mobile phone. "A few discreet questions and I should also be able to discover what sort of laboratory facilities they have on site. It will be a good indication of how much longer after closing hours their staff would stay to run tests."

Both Tristan and Lucas frowned at her as she punched in the numbers from the letterhead on the files. She waved a hand to keep them quiet and put on her perkiest voice as the receptionist answered the call.

"Good afternoon," Kimber said. "I've got some rudimentary blood tests that I need done. I was wondering if I booked in to see one of your GPs how long it would take?"

"You'd need to have a regular consultation," the receptionist explained, her tone and the fast pace of her words indicating she'd gone through this many times. "One of the nurses on staff can take the sample immediately after your appointment. If it's one of the tests we can do on sight the turnaround time is usually twenty-four to forty-eight hours, but if there are any further tests we usually have those taken care of by a consulting laboratory off site. Would you like to make an appointment?"

"What are your opening hours again please?"

"We're open from eight a.m. until seven p.m. Monday to Friday and from nine until three on Saturdays," the receptionist parroted.

"Okay, I'll give you a call back if I need an appointment," Kimber replied. "Thank you so much for your help."

"My pleasure. Good day."

Kimber hung up feeling satisfied.

"They have a lab but I bet it's a fairly fundamental one. Probably a half-dozen staff at any given time.

Their turnaround time for simplistic tests is one to two days, so that means there's not a regular night shift that I can tell. They close at seven."

Tristan and Lucas stood up and moved to a large map of London that was hung on the wall.

"The clinic is on the corner here," Tristan said as he indicated a spot on the map to Lucas. "If we park across the street here we should be able to mingle in the market crowd from here and still be able to monitor people coming and leaving."

"I was talking to Olasis in the tech department the other day," Lucas added, excitement in his voice. "He bragged how they now have eavesdropping devices that can automatically filter out ambient noise from up to three hundred yards. A pair of those babies would be perfect for this."

"Do you think you can borrow a pair from him?" Tristan asked. Kimber stood and came over to their map.

The men discussed other various pieces of equipment they would need to gather. She only half listened. Studying the map, she didn't see anything helpful she could add at this time and so remained silent.

"I'll go gather it all now," Lucas' voice interrupted her thoughts. Kimber looked up as he winked mischievously at her. "We'll meet in the car park around six, right?"

"How long do you plan to chat up the girls in technology?" Tristan asked, the grin belying the verbal poke.

Lucas shook his head and laughed, slapping Tristan's shoulder.

"Your mind is in the gutter, my man. I planned to grab a quick bite to eat. It might be a long night. You two have fun now, you hear?"

Tristan chuckled. The men shook hands. Lucas sketched a quick wave to Kimber before leaving the room. She felt a warm beginning of friendship blossoming with the man, but it was the dark-haired agent left behind who really got her blood stirred up. Kimberly shared a soft smile with him as he turned to face her fully.

The last few hours still seemed surreal to her. While the events so far hadn't occured like in a movie — all action and guns blazing, buildings exploding and cars chasing — the elusive undercurrent of adventure hung in the air for her. Add on the strong undercurrent of sexual awareness and she felt like she'd been through enough foreplay for the day.

"I guess we should go get kitted out," Tristan murmured, his voice thick with lust.

Anticipation had her nipples beading. The sensual rasp of her delicate tips straining against the lacy cups of her bra and the soft linen of her business shirt heightened her need unbearably.

Her throat felt too dry for her to speak, so she merely nodded. Part of her mind wondered what kind of kit they'd need to break into a building, the other half of her remained focused on how soon they could spare a moment alone so she could take control of her rising need and kiss this man silly. It took only a matter of moments for them to collect the files, arrange them into a neat pile again and leave the conference room. Tristan deposited the mountain of paperwork on a desk as they passed — she assumed it was his table — and they left the large, open-plann office area and walked into the corridor.

Tristan pushed open the door to the stairwell then glanced at her over his shoulder.

"It's only a flight of stairs down and the lifts take forever around here," he explained.

Kimber glanced down at her low-heeled shoes and shrugged.

"A bit of exercise will be good for me," she reassured him.

Tristan gallantly held the door for her and she entered the dim stairwell. She walked down the first few steps, jumping when the door thudded closed behind them with a dull bang.

"Claustrophobic?" Tristan asked.

She paused and tilted her head to look at him as she spoke.

"No, I'm just edgy and the noise took me by surprise."

Tristan walked to the stair below her then turned so he was facing her. In that brief instant Kimber felt her breath catch in her throat. The difference in height had been removed by her standing a step higher than Tristan. Not giving herself a moment to overthink her actions, she cupped a hand to the side of his jaw and drew their mouths together.

Passion shook through her body at the soft, sensual contact. Tristan's lips were soft and warm, the heat radiating out from his body in the narrow stairwell. Time froze for one perfect second as they came together. It was like her whole life had been leading up to this very action.

Gasping at the intensity of the simple, chaste kiss, Kimber tilted her head so they could continue to press together, but she could part her lips infinitesimally and draw a quick breath.

"No," Tristan murmured. He snaked his hand out to clasp her hip and draw her full body flush with his.

"Don't go yet," he spoke raggedly, clearly as affected as she. "I need this so much. You've been driving me crazy up there. My head was full of these images while I couldn't do anything about it, in front of Lucas and everyone."

Kimber could only moan before she fused their lips together once again. This time she made her hands busy as well. No longer was she imposing herself upon this sexy man, his actions and words spoke clearly. He wanted this as much as she did.

Free to explore as she willed, Kimber traced her hands lightly down his jaw line over the warm column of his neck. Shivers racked her body as his hands cupped her ass through the thinness of her skirt. Canting her hips up to rub herself wantonly over his hard erection, Kimber could barely believe these actions were hers.

Hers—laboratory geek—Kimber!

She had never been more appreciative of her mother's advice to always wear nice underwear. This morning she had already felt like a spy and had put on her raunchiest aqua, lacy thong. Kimber moaned decadently as Tristan ran his hand up and under her skirt, her legs wobbled as he traced the soft pads of his fingers tenderly over her flesh and hooked them inside her knickers.

"So hot," he murmured. "So wet."

Kimber lifted one leg up around his waist to open herself more fully to him. Staring into his hot, dark brown gaze she felt lost in the exhilaration. They continued to press their lips against one another, opening their mouths so they could tangle their tongues hotly together.

Tasting faintly of bitter coffee and sensual maleness, he was a potent elixir to her system.

Tristan muffled a groan. He turned them both to the side and pressed her back into the cool concrete wall of the stairwell. Heat seared her as he caressed his fingers over her swollen pussy lips, her juices coating him in a slick sheen.

Arching her back, she pressed herself onto him, the ache inside her body like a physical blow.

"I need you," she panted, "I've never wanted anyone this badly or so much ever before."

Tristan grunted, stroked the tender folds of her heated entrance and thrust three long fingers deeply inside her throbbing cunt. Kimber groaned, she felt fantastically full. He stretched her and pumped his digits into her very depths. He plundered her over and over. Kimber's stomach knotted with pleasure. Her heartbeat raced, her eyes fluttered shut as her body blossomed and opened to him.

She'd never had sex with a man less than a few hours after meeting him, nor even after the first date. Yet nothing could stop her now. She was on an adventure, excitement was her middle name, she was very nearly a spy in her own thriller mystery movie and—

The sound of a door groaning and heavy wood moving split the air. Quick as a wink Tristan turned them again so his body was protectively between her and the door to the corridor above. With his back to the entry Tristan smoothly but hastily withdrew his fingers from the depths of her body, twitched the hem of her skirt back down to flirt with her knees and turned around. A willowy redhead came into view just as Tristan nudged Kimber into continuing down the stairs.

They both looked up and Kimber had to fight the urge not to laugh aloud. Seconds too late, the woman looked down at them, two innocuous business workers walking down a flight of stairs for a spot of exercise instead of waiting for the lift.

Nothing to see here.

They nodded in silent greeting to each other. Tristan and Kimberly reached the door to the floor below and once again Tristan opened it for her. Murmuring her thanks, she entered the corridor and could hardly believe the explosive passion from a moment before had been real. Indeed, the whole day appeared fantastical, something simply happening in her mind or to someone else entirely.

"Our kit lockers are down this hall, last door to the left," Tristan said. He raised a hand to indicate the hall. As he did so, his left hand brushed hers, electricity sparkling between them at the touch. Her gaze clashed with his, hot brown melting her to the core.

Wickedly, he lifted his right hand—the fingers which had penetrated her—and slowly licked them one by one.

For the first time since they'd been together Kimber felt her face flaming in a hot, dark blush. She cast a panicked look left, then right, checking to make sure no one stood around to watch his decadent display.

No one in their right minds could mistake his meaning of what he had just tasted. Thankfully there was not a soul in sight.

"Creamy and feminine with just a hint of spice," he said in a sultry whisper. "Exactly like you, Kimber."

She felt conflicted. Part of her desperately wanted to pick up exactly where they had left off, but common decency reared its ugly head. Throwing caution to the wind—uncaring of how quickly this had all happened—Kimber pressed her body hard against the muscled line of his. Heat radiated from his skin, branding her even through both their clothes. She kissed him passionately, sucked his tongue deeply into her mouth in ardent promise.

Wrenching herself away—for if she had remained there for another second she'd have shed her clothes and outright begged him to take her there and then— she strode towards the door he had indicated. Kimber guessed she had read thousands of spy thriller novels and probably seen over a couple of hundred movies. Nothing could have prepared her for what the reality turned out to be.

Chapter Three

Kimber entered an enormous room with a linoleum floor. Eight-foot-tall lockers took up the far wall, many of them with stickers, names and padlocks on them. A few of the doors remained open, seeming to be communal, or perhaps temporary lockers for those who might need them.

Racks of general items filled a large portion of the space. Batteries, communication units, a large plastic tub full of mobile phones. Kimber only had a second to scan the area, noting as she did that it was empty of people. Thick, warm arms were wrapped around her.

She turned into the embrace, her eyes fluttering shut. Tristan pushed his mouth onto hers. They feasted upon each other as if they were starved. Tristan drove a hand into her curls, gently tugging the hair tie out and murmuring softly when her hair fell down just past her shoulders.

"I've never had a preference before," he said, "but now I am definitely a curls man. Blonde curls."

Kimber wrapped her arms around his shoulders, drawing him even closer. Tristan leaned into her so far she had to bend back slightly to counter his weight. She tugged on his shirt then pushed the top few buttons from their holes. With his help she managed to lift the entire item from his body. He shrugged out of it and the linen fell into a crumpled heap onto the floor.

Lightly she traced her fingers over his chest, the hard muscles of his pecs smooth and warm to her touch. His small, nut-brown nipples were hard nubs, his skin slightly tanned. Curious and eager to explore, Kimberly leant forwards so she could move her lips along the smooth expanse of his skin.

She grazed her mouth over him, flicking her tongue out to taste him.

"Mmm," she murmured. She moved, licked him again, rasped over his nipple. Delighted when this action elicited a low groan from him, she chuckled. Emboldened, she repeated the gesture, a startled gasp of laughter falling from her lips as he lifted her up, turned her around and pressed her into the hard, cold brick of the nearest stretch of wall.

"Tristan!" she called out. Exasperation laced her shout. She felt a small measure of indignation at being manhandled as easily as a toy, but was unable to deny the fierce surge of lust the enticing move had caused within her.

She lifted her hands instinctively to push herself away, but the solid heat of Tristan's body pressed into her back. Kimber felt breathless again as he ground his thick, hard erection into the curve of her arse. Ensnared by him, she shifted back, shimmying against him as they danced erotically together.

Tristan wrapped an arm around her. He tugged her pencil-slim skirt up with his other hand, letting it bunch at her waist. Turning her head to glance at him, she found Tristan staring down her body with hot, ravenous dark eyes.

"An aqua lace thong?" he choked out. He he raised his eyebrows, lust hot in his gaze.

She grinned.

"And a matching demi-cup bra," she purred, thrilled to witness such an intense reaction.

He moved the arm from her waist, his hand twisting at the wrist so he could pull the hem of her knitted sleeveless vest. In two quick motions Kimber shed both the vest and her shirt. Turning to face him, she stood in the large room, feeling safe in the warm circle of his embrace. She took a deep breath, swelling her small breasts so they filled the lacy matching bra. The demi-cup lifted her, showcasing her cleavage and setting her off to advantage.

Tristan ran the pads of his fingers over the curve of one mound, touching her as if she were a mirage and would disappear the moment he held her fully. The surreal nature of the moment crashed over Kimber. Never in her wildest flights of fancy could she have even imagined something like this happening to her. She reached out to cup Tristan's jaw and kiss him once again, half certain the action would shatter the illusion and she'd wake up, cold and alone in her bed.

There was no jerk of waking up. No cruel alarm clock or laboratory timer to buzz and interrupt her fantasy. This was the real deal.

Heat met her touch, her tongue tangled with his, the wet strength giving back as good as she was giving. Her heart pounded in her chest and the realisation that she was about to have steamy, raunchy sex with a man she'd met mere hours ago finally sank in.

Holy fuck, she was really about to do this.

Still kissing him fiercely, Kimberly reached for the waist of Tristan's pants. Fumbling only for a moment with the unfamiliar clasp, she wrestled to free the heated shaft she felt pressing against her body.

Tristan broke away from their kiss with a muted curse, helping her push both his pants and boxers down his thighs. Swearing in earnest he dipped one arm down into the pocket of his pants, withdrew his wallet and dug a condom out of it. With his other hand he gently nudged her around again. Willingly she turned, heard the crinkle of foil and shivered as warm fingers probed beneath her thong once again.

Together they removed the tiny scrap of lace, Kimber wobbling as she balanced on one leg then the other to step out of the knickers, and finally, she widened her stance as Tristan urged her legs apart and settled his thick head against her pussy entrance.

"Are you certain?" he whispered raggedly against her ear.

Kimber lifted her hands up, pressed them against the wall for balance. With her legs spread wide for balance she moaned at the delicious feel of Tristan's cock seated right there where she could feel its heat soak into her pussy lips. Her juices flowed and blood thrummed in her ear, her head pounding for him to just do it, for fuck's sake. She could hardly believe this sweet man held himself together by an inch to reassure himself she was willing.

"Tristan Walters," she panted, "if you don't fuck me right now, hard and up against this wall, I will find a gun on one of these shelves and shoot you myself."

Heat penetrated her, a tight stretching as he took her at her word and sheathed his thick cock deeply into her cunt. Kimber arched her back, her breasts pressing against the cool bricks as she canted her hips back to take even more of him.

"Oh yes!" she hissed, not having the breath to cry out or say more.

She whimpered as Tristan withdrew, the aching loss of him unbelievable after the warmth and fullness of his penetration. She cried out in bliss as he rammed back into her once again.

In and out, over and over he sawed into her. Each time her walls clenched tightly, clamping down over him, greedily sucking him deeper and deeper.

"More," she moaned, lost in the thick fog of her passion.

Tristan lowered his head to the curve of her shoulder and bit gently down into the tender spot right there. The painful sensation drove her pleasure higher, spiking their lovemaking like a shot of liquor into her drink.

Pressing her arse back, Kimber panted. Tristan moved harder and faster. She felt her walls stretching, struggling to encompass his full width as he pounded into her body. Arching up, the stunning blend of hunger and pain heightened her senses. Adrenaline coursed through her and the knot of sensual need curled deep in her stomach grew.

Reaching an arm around, Kimber grabbed her lover's thigh, her blunt nails digging slightly into the tight flesh of his cheeks. Tristan grunted, nipped another biting kiss to the slender column of her neck and pumped inside her clenching channel again. Panting, she struggled to find a coherent word to urge him on. Her mind muddled, language escaped her.

Besides, she couldn't catch her breath even had she known what to say.

"Oh!" she moaned as Tristan lowered a hand to stroke tenderly at her clit. Her body shuddered, tightened and for a perilous moment she tottered on the very edge of climax.

"Come for me, baby," he crooned to her, sensuality dripping from his every syllable. Her hand twitched, tightened around his buttock and her nails bit a little into the tender flesh.

With a scream, Kimber flew apart, her world shattering. Her pussy clenched tight around Tristan's thick cock. Milking him, she shuddered over and over. Before her contractions had finished his hips jerked, short spasms rocking through him. He pumped into her, emptying himself into the thin latex.

Lungs bellowing, the harsh sounds of strangled breath filled the room as they both came down from the monumental climax. Kimber turned her head, leaning slightly to the side so she could gaze upon her lover.

Tiny beads of sweat dotted his brow, his head hung down, his fringe almost falling into his eyes. Kimber lifted a hand, running her fingers through the soft strands, enjoying the contrast between their darkness and the light of her digits. At her touch Tristan lifted his eyes to meet hers. She smiled warmly, desire, lust and a tenderness she hadn't expected filling her chest while they silently watched each other.

"Am I a real spy now?" she asked.

As she had hoped, the potentially awkward moment passed and Tristan chuckled. Twisting one of her curls around his index finger, he tugged the strand to his lips, kissing it before letting it spring free from its bondage.

"I'm not sure that qualifies," he replied. "But I'm certain if you have your way before the evening is through you will be a bona fide spy. Breaking and entering a facility isn't the usual method of initiation, but that seems to be the path you're determined to follow."

Kimber cupped his jaw and drew Tristan near to press their lips together one final time in benediction. Heat flared between them and his cock twitched with interest within her body.

Groaning in dismay, he pulled his shaft out of her.

"We were lucky no one came last time," he insisted. "Neither of our reputations would survive someone walking in on us here."

Part of her—the wild, wicked section she'd never noticed before let alone indulged in—wanted to insist they live in the moment and give in to their passions. The logical part of her brain, however, urged sense and caution. Bending down to collect her shirt and vest, Kimber went about setting herself to rights once more.

Tristan pulled his clothes back into order and moved to his locker. Pulling a handful of tissues from a travel pack he cleaned himself and disposed of the used condom. Giving them both a moment to compose themselves, Kimber pulled herself together, then turned to him with a radiant smile.

"So, what do we pack into a spy's kit?"

* * * *

Kimber sat on a bench near the lockers and watched as Tristan placed item after item in a medium-sized duffel bag. Already she had needed to ask what a number of the items were, finding herself surprised at his responses. A small zippered case which had reminded her of a lady's manicure set had turned out to be a very professional-looking set of lock picks.

Tristan collected what appeared to be a thick fountain pen and popped it into his pocket.

"Oh, I have a collection of pens in my handbag back upstairs," she replied.

Tristan paused in the act of coiling up a long length of rope to gaze at her. Her breath caught as her body reacted to the handsome sight he made.

"Oh love, you're such a sweet, innocent little thing," he commented, half laughing, half serious.

She scowled, but couldn't think of a comeback quickly enough.

Twisting the rope deftly he knotted the length into an easily-removable knot and packed it into the duffel.

Tristan removed the pen and held it out to her. After a pause, realising he meant for her to take it, she picked it from his fingers and turned it over. She studied it for a few seconds before giving up and looking back to him. She shrugged, perplexed. "Okay. Impress me, lover. What is it? There's no chamber or room for a bullet, so it isn't a gun. A taser, maybe? Oh! No, I know. It's a camera, right? The new must-have toy for perverted youths to up-skirt unsuspecting women on the train at night."

Tristan chuckled and shook his head, a brief, sharp motion. "An excellent idea, darling," he replied, seeming to enjoy himself. "But no. It's a scanner."

Kimber turned the pen over a few times in her hand, staring hard at it. She gaped, wondered how such a slender, relatively small object could hide such technology then held it out for him to take back.

"You're kidding me. Really?"

She watched, enthralled, as he pressed the end and aimed the nib onto her hand. A thin laser dot appeared.

"Point, click and hey presto, it scans and holds images, photos, paintings and anything written. Holds up to eight gigabytes of data before you need to exchange the cartridge with a new memory card."

"Wow," she breathed.

"I'll add a small digital camera into our bag, too," he reassured her, "but this pen is not only discreet, but should be faster and safer than having to line up endless papers and put them in the right light to photograph. The laser can pick up writing in only forty per cent light and adjusts itself accordingly. Any photos we find will need at least sixty per cent light to come out clearly, but I'm hoping most of the data we want to copy and recover will be reports on whatever the hell Henley had going in this operation."

"What will happen to her if I uncover something really bad?" Kimber asked, apprehensive for the first time. She'd been so focused on helping Preston and playing at being a spy she hadn't really thought through the full ramifications of the work she was undertaking. Tristan shook his head angrily, brushing off her concern.

"Emma Henley is a traitor and a murderer," he said curtly, his gaze cast down at the pen in his hands. "She abused the privilege of this office, used the tools and personnel under her protection and involved herself with terrorists. She is directly responsible for two deaths, one of them being my old partner. He had a family, a sister who still calls me periodically to tearfully recount stories to help work through her grief."

Kimber fell silent, almost not breathing. The pain Tristan so clearly felt had been put aside, but was not even close to being forgotten or settled.

"I'm sorry," she spoke softly.

He took a deep breath and tilted his head in acknowledgement, then shook himself as if to physically cast off the sombre moment.

"Henley is already neck-deep in shit. She'll never see the light of day again. In a sense she is secondary to all this. It's merely this is her project, the audit of her work that has drawn us to this place. She has enough sins cast at her door to atone for. What we want to know is whether there is something for us to clean up here, or whether we're jumping at shadows and being paranoid."

Kimber nodded. She certainly didn't feel better for having had this explained to her, but at least she knew now she would not be responsible for casting a slur upon an innocent party.

"Do we have time for me to pop home and change?" she asked hopefully. She craved a brief shower to clean up and didn't relish the thought of doing her first round of breaking and entering in a business shirt, pencil-slim skirt and low heels. With a wry grin she thought fondly of decking herself out in head-to-toe black — much like every thief she'd ever seen in the movies.

"Much as I hate to think of a black beanie covering those beautiful blonde curls, darling, yes, I think we will both need a fresh outfit," Tristan acknowledged. "Let's wrap up here, go back up and talk to Lucas before we collect your bag and then we can swing by both our places really quickly."

"Won't Lucas need to change too?" she asked, curious.

Tristan grinned at her in reply. He looked sensually wicked, like a boy with a naughty plan in mind.

"Lucas has seen my flat more often than he needs to. Nor do I relish the thought of sharing my first experience at your place with him, brief though it will have to be. We can meet him at an all-night shop I know of nearby. We can all grab a quick bite to eat and then stake the clinic out in comfort and not have to listen to the growls of our stomachs."

Kimber closed the distance between them and pressed a warm, searching kiss to Tristan's lips. He wrapped well-muscled arms tightly around her waist, drawing her near to him. She reached up to thread her fingers through his soft, dark hair and their kiss deepened hungrily.

They both made appreciative sounds, exploring one another at leisure, when the door opened and the sound of heavy footfalls entered the room. Kimber stepped back, her lips and body burning where she could still sense the weight of Tristan's touch. She took a deep breath of air and smiled at him.

"Like I said," Tristan said, lust thick in his tone. "We might have to be quick in my flat—or yours—but no way am I sharing that with Lucas."

She chuckled as they finished packing the duffel, eager as he was to get moving.

Chapter Four

Night had covered the city, wrapping it within its dark embrace. They had a clear view of the clinic and adjacent medical facility from the black pool car. Kimber, Tristan and Lucas had witnessed a mass exodus of receptionists and laboratory staff about quarter past seven in the evening. Three doctors had dashed out of the building less than five minutes past the hour.

The city streetlights burned in the inky-black evening and Kimber had to keep on reminding herself not to jiggle with barely repressed eagerness. After the second time she'd asked whether they could go in, the indulgent looks both Tristan and Lucas had cast her way had made her feel like a child eager to go on the first fair ride.

At least I hadn't asked if we're there yet, she consoled herself.

"Can I at least have a brief walk around the building?" she said, pleased to hear only faint impatience and not a hint of whine in her tone.

Tristan chuckled and shook his head without a word.

"Actually I almost suggested I do that," Lucas replied with a quick glance to his partner.

Kimber opened her mouth, about to insist she go with him, but quickly snapped it shut again.

Tristan and Lucas were the professionals here. Not her. When they entered the laboratory or were discussing scientific papers and hypotheses her knowledge became greater than theirs. In this instance, she needed to follow their lead, even if she did chafe to enjoy her grand adventure.

She remained silent while Tristan cast a curious glance towards Lucas. Her lover didn't speak a word, evidently happy for Lucas to explain his reasoning. Kimber watched as Lucas appeared to collect his thoughts together before putting forth his argument.

"For starters, since you and Kimberly are the ones who will be breaking in, I think it would look terribly suspicious if you're caught on CCTV casing the joint," he replied earnestly. "Not to mention the fact if there is surveillance of any kind, having a clear picture of your face will lead the cops right to the Agency's doorstep. Worse, if they have Kimber's description or identification as a civilian you'll be in a hell of a lot more trouble than either of us."

Kimber wrinkled her nose in distaste at this thought.

"This way, I can wander around looking innocent, get an idea of what you'll both be up against and see if the coast is clear for tonight's shenanigans to begin. It will also give me a chance to see if I can use this," Lucas finished as he pulled what looked like a security key pass from the inner pocket of his jacket. The small card looked unprepossessing and Kimber pondered if — much like the pen and other gadgets Tristan had explained to her earlier—it was actually something more than a regular pass.

"I brought lock picks," Tristan replied with an uneasy glance to the building before returning his attention to the small card. "This is supposed to be a small, privately run clinic."

"Even without drugs on the premises places like these go overboard on their security nowadays," Lucas insisted. "Hell, my local veterinary clinic has its own external security guards on patrol through the weekends. It was the only thing they could do to slow down the rates of break-ins."

Lucas threw a happy grin over his shoulder to her and explained, "Lock picks might be old-fashioned but are perfect for once you get inside and disarm the security system. But I'm willing to bet you'll need this baby to get in the front door. I'll walk around, find out which company the clinic uses for their electronic system and it will only take a quick call to our IT people to be able to programme you both an access key."

He patted at his inner jacket pocket. It revealed to Kimber the outline of a small box, a little bigger than a pack of cigarettes. "How do you know your IT department will be able to guess exactly which system is used?" she asked.

Her curiosity had started to fight with a strange case of nerves. Much of the surreal nature of this day had bled into the realisation that this really wasn't a game, that she was about to break any number of laws and possibly get herself into some very hot water.

Excitement at the thrill of her first adventure warred with her usually cautious nature.

"Okay, big shot," Tristan replied with a grin. The two men bumped fists before Lucas left the car.

Kimber laced her fingers together and took a deep breath.

"You don't have to do this," Tristan spoke softly in the darkness. She heard him turn around and face her. The dim lamplight glowed orange, casting his face half in shadow, half in light. Black suited him. A knitted black sweater with dark jeans complemented his lean frame, tanned skin and dark hair.

Kimber looked down to her own grey denims and black long-sleeved shirt. It was the closest she'd found in her closet to what her idea of thief clothes would look like. Gathering her courage, she reminded herself this was almost precisely what she had daydreamed and fantasised about for years.

She would never forgive herself if she chickened out at the first hint of nerves.

"Definitely not," she replied more firmly than she had intended. Softening her tone she continued, "I'm not sure it's something I can explain fully to you. Your life is full of danger and excitement and the very sure knowledge you're making a difference protecting lives and saving our country and world practically on a daily basis." She struggled to put words to her feelings.

"When I was in school, studying diseases and vaccines, I was like dozens of other students. I wanted to save the world, cure cancer, heal the sick and make everything right. Towards the end of that time it slowly but inevitably dawned on me there are only so many positions like that. Most people are perfectly ordinary and while they might be good people, working in good jobs, it's only the rare case who gets to achieve what I dreamed of. So in the large part I settled for normal and stable, put my dreams out of my working life and went about my regular days."

Kimber met Tristan's gaze, staring at him and willing him to understand.

"Despite all that, I couldn't leave my dreams behind, I craved an adventure, and in my heart I still want to save people, it's been my secret practically forever. Preston coming to me, even being able to help in part on this mission, it's what I've always wanted and all day it has felt very surreal to me. It's like I'm an actor playing a part. Reality and ramifications didn't seem to apply to me, or at least, they hadn't sunk in until about five minutes ago."

She grinned, wanting to lighten the heaviness of her confession. Tristan continued to stare at her, his dark gaze penetrating to her very core. He nodded.

"I won't let anything happen to you."

Kimber couldn't help but smile at the serious tone in his voice, as if his words were an oath, sworn in blood and meant down to his soul. She hadn't ever felt so cherished and protected in her many, many years. She tilted her head, much of her good humour returning at his promise.

"I know," she replied. "I'm not scared exactly. It's more as if the reality is starting to bleed through and merging with the fantasy. It's a bit nerve-racking, but I'm still loving every moment I have with this."

"Are you certain you don't want to back out?" Tristan pressed. "I can scan all the documents and send them to you here in the car. You don't need to be in danger, to put your life in jeopardy, to be helpful. I understand how much this means to you. Any fool would have worked it out by now and I think your excitement has breathed fresh life into both my and Lucas' desire to do this job."

Kimber scooted forward on the rear car seat, reached out and took Tristan's hand with hers. He squeezed her fingers gently and she felt a rush of warmth and love pour through her. She knew he wasn't trying to force her out of this mission, but merely trying to protect her. The gesture meant a lot and solidified the growing knowledge that that he was a good man, a warrior and protector at heart. She knew her safety was in capable hands with him.

"Nothing could persuade me to back out now," she said far more bravely than her stomach felt. "With Lucas playing guard dog and you by my side what could possibly go wrong?"

"Words to never say before you go into the pit." Tristan chuckled.

Her heart raced as he lifted her knuckles to his lips and pressed a hot kiss to her skin. Moving herself against the back of the front seat, she reached out her other hand and stroked the back of her fingers along the soft skin of his jaw. Faint stubble rasped. She shivered with delight at the sensation.

"This isn't a pit," she teased, laughter clear in her tone. "This is a grand adventure. We're going to find the bad guy, save the world and bring peace and harmony to—"

"Oh hell," Tristan groaned, reluctant laughter chuckling from his chest. "Saints save me from those rose-tinted glasses you continue to wear."

Laughing, Kimber lifted herself to close the distance between her and Tristan and planted a hot, fast kiss to his lips. She sat back down and ran her fingers through her hair to collect the stray curls back into a ponytail.

"You don't fool me anymore, Walters," she insisted, half serious, half teasing. "You love it. I'm not taken in by that jaded-old-man routine you try to bamboozle

Lucas and the others with. At heart you want to save the world too. I can tell."

Tristan snorted but didn't refute her comment. He stared at her a moment in silence before shrugging and turning to glance out the windshield. Kimber caught a tiny twitch of a smile at the corner of his mouth before he hid the reaction from her.

"Don't go spreading that around, love. You're going to ruin my reputation you know."

"I don't think anyone important is going to worry about it," she said. "Lucas certainly seems to think you're an excellent role model."

Before Tristan could reply they both caught sight of the young man returning. Edgy excitement pooled in her stomach once again when she realised this was probably it. She was finally going to dash from the blocks and begin the experience of a lifetime.

Silence filled the car as Lucas opened the door and climbed into the passenger seat. The door slammed shut behind him and he turned to watch them both.

"Done and dusted," he spoke cheerily, handing over the security pass. "IT didn't even need to search the system, they use the same company HQ does. I barely had to use my special skills to copy the card."

"So this will get us inside?" Tristan checked and pocketed the card.

"Yeah, mate. If you circle around back you both should miss the security cameras. I noticed a side entrance which seems to be for deliveries, there's a biohazard sign on the door. It's just off a tiny alley, so I presume it's where the lab pick-ups come and go."

"I usually broadcast on the open channel." Tristan fiddled with his communication piece in his ear.

Kimber watched, entranced.

"That sounds fine, and it will be perfect if we need to call in more support."

Tristan glared at Lucas.

"What happened to Mr Optimistic? It will be easy, a quick in and out." Tristan mocked Lucas' earlier words.

Lucas laughed, unconcerned.

"Just covering our arses, mate."

Kimber's stomach clenched for a second time as Tristan lifted his sweater to settle the large handgun at the base of his spine. Appearing content with the weapon's position he pulled the clothing back down to cover it and picked up the duffel with all their gear in it. Almost as an afterthought he pulled the security card from his pocket and handed it back to Kimber.

"Here, love, you keep this."

She took it then glanced to his duffel and his concealed gun.

"Shouldn't I hold the bag? Won't you need your hands free?"

"I can juggle this," Tristan asserted.

"At the first hint of trouble you use that card to run straight back out here," Lucas cautioned her. Tristan's actions suddenly came into much clearer focus. She held the card stiffly back out to Tristan.

"I'm not going to leave you in there," she insisted. He put a palm out to push the card and her hand away from him.

"Just hold onto it," he cajoled her. "If something goes wrong I'll need to cover our flank. I can't do that and swipe the card simultaneously. You'll need to do that."

The spike of her anger cooled at his logical explanation.

"Oh," she said, deflated. "Well, okay then."

"Last chance to back out." Tristan turned and rested his hand on the handle, pausing just before he opened the car door.

"Nope, you're stuck with me." She smirked.

"We'll be back," Tristan said over his shoulder to Lucas.

"I'll be here, keep me apprised over the comms."

Kimber climbed out of the car with a final backward glance to Lucas through the window. She came shoulder to shoulder with Tristan while they walked down the street. Silently, they passed the building and crossed the road three doors down from their target.

"Stick with me," Tristan said in a quiet, commanding voice. "Just follow my lead."

Kimber nodded, her heart thundering, blood pounding in her ears. The night seemed to open up before her as her senses heightened with the adrenaline spiking her system. The darkness wasn't so complete, her night vision having adjusted. She heard the sounds of nearby cars, people talking a block or so away as well as the distant beat of music from a pub or club.

Glancing nervously around, she checked to make sure no one was nearby to notice them.

"Keep looking ahead of us," Tristan cautioned her. "Lucas and I will both keep a discreet eye out. We need to appear normal. Acting oddly will only draw attention to us."

The sudden warmth of Tristan's hand encompassing her own took her by surprise. For an instant Kimber had to catch herself before she jumped or pulled away. Only a split second later she relaxed against Tristan, soaking up the strength he silently offered her. Hand in hand they turned down the small driveway-cum-alley beside the building as if it was the most natural place in the world for them to be walking in the dark of night.

Without hurrying they walked to the side door, noticing the small biohazard caution sign indicating low levels of pathogen waste could be found inside.

"Hold on a second," Tristan said half under his breath as he released her hand. He dug two pairs of thin leather gloves out of the duffel. Without another word he handed her a pair and quickly pulled them on.

Following his lead, Kimber tugged the gloves onto her hands, adjusting the fingers so she could retain most of her dexterity.

A card scanner was at hand height next to the handle. Excitement mounting as Tristan nodded silently for her to proceed, Kimber swiped the card. The tiny LED swapped from red to green, a discreet beep indicating they'd bypassed the system.

Tristan opened the door and ducked his head inside. After a quick glance up and down he moved sideways, bracing himself to block the entrance open. He indicated with a tilt of his head for her to enter first. Kimber moved inside the doorway a few steps then paused to gather her bearings.

She had come into a long, dimly lit corridor. The outer door closed with a low *thunk* behind Tristan.

"We're in," he said.

Kimber frowned and turned to him, about to reply that of course they were inside, but she quickly understood he was speaking into his unit to let Lucas know what was going on.

Light came through from the far end of the corridor. Kimber walked towards it, confident in leading the way now they were effectively in her world.

"I would think the lab would be around the back here somewhere, probably with the nurses' station where they draw blood or give vaccines."

"Should we search the filing cabinets as well?" Tristan asked as he followed a half pace behind her. Kimber shook her head, frowning thoughtfully.

"If the nurses or other laboratory staff do their own testing they should have a cabinet or area near their desks to keep their reports in," she answered. She slowly depressed the handle and cracked it open.

Half expecting an alarm to sound or for someone to shout at her, she paused with the door open just a few millimetres. When no sound broke through the air except for their own quick breaths, Kimber sighed in relief and opened it fully.

In a small antechamber were vaccination posters as well as general medical health and wellbeing posters colourfully displayed on the walls. A large calendar had small, handwritten notations in shorthand on many of the days. A small plaque half hidden under a pile of paperwork in the inbox on one corner of the large desk stated—'Nurses are patient people'.

Kimber smiled at the pun.

An open entrance at the other end of the antechamber showed what Kimber assumed was the laboratory area. Moving into the room, and without touching anything, she took the cramped space in a glance. She noted from the corner of her eye Tristan closed the door to the corridor behind them. Cords on the table indicated a computer had been removed for the evening—presumably a laptop the nurses used to keep their appointments on and connect to the network of online medical files and patient data.

Requests for testing, however, always had to be printed out in hard copy and signed, as did laboratory results.

"Shall we start with the nurses' station?" Kimber asked as she tested the filing cabinet next to the desk.

Locked.

"I just want to check the lab is clear, first," Tristan said in a soft tone as he passed her and moved cautiously through the open door.

Kimber looked for the cabinet key, fairly certain it would be nearby. With casual staff, temporary staff and everyone presumably on rotation throughout the days and weeks it wasn't logical that there would be more than a few copies of the cabinet key. It would be far more likely for there to be one communal key for the majority of staff to use and it would have to be kept in easy grabbing distance.

After checking on top of the filing cabinet, under the potted plant on the desk and on the carpet either side of the cabinet she opened the top drawer of the desk. It was clearly a 'junk' drawer. She was greeted by pens scattered everywhere, sticky notes, a half-filled box of tea bags, numerous latex gloves and an assortment of astounding proportions of day-to-day debris.

In one corner under a pile of over-the-counter, low-strength painkillers were two shiny keys on a ring.

"Ha!" she crowed, amazingly proud of this small achievement. When Kimber tested the key in the lock it fit perfectly and turned easily.

Tristan returned as she pulled open the top drawer. She threw him a brilliant smile, riding high on the thrill of success.

"This is awesome fun," she gushed. "Do you think we'll get really lucky and find a folder titled Project Immunity?"

"I doubt it," he replied before kissing her forehead. "But you know what they say about beginners' luck. Budge over a bit so I can see too. Do you have that list, love?"

While they prepared themselves for this very moment, Tristan had jotted down the list of nine names from the folders Emma Henley had copied. Kimber felt certain she could recall them all, but Tristan had insisted that they write them out.

"You'd be astonished how oddly people react to a small thing like breaking and entering," he had warned her. "In the heat of the moment people forget their own names, let alone small details like this. It's better to have everything organised as much as possible. That way you keep errors to a minimum."

Kimber pulled the scrap of paper out of the back pocket of her jeans and read the names aloud.

"Jeremy Bowmen, Karol Oldfield, Olive Carragher, Ennis Farlough, Talone Ondra, Abigail Turner, Asher Wevell, Dolores Kienl, Mather Niese."

"Right. You take Neil through to Talone and I'll take Abigail through to Mather," Tristan said as he bent to the task of searching the records.

Kimber placed the paper on the corner of the desk where they could both see the neatly printed names. Struck by an idea, she pulled a random file out to make certain it was personal files. She opened 'Alcock, Jean'.

A hasty mental calculation told her the fifty-seven-year-old mother of four had most recently had her flu vaccination along with her annual pap smear four months ago here at the nurses' station. After putting the file away she then pulled out another quickly, to confirm her suspicions.

'Brandy, Steve' had last been in three years ago according to the notation and had had blood drawn for an iron and haemoglobin count as well as a general battery of tests like cholesterol and blood glucose levels.

His sample had been contracted out and the official report was stapled behind the doctor's standard form, which encompassed the request for testing—but which didn't include any of the doctor's consultations or notes.

"These are just the nurse's records," she explained. "These will all be the copies of requests for testing, vaccinations, anything the nurses themselves do."

"Oh. Well it can't hurt to look while we're here," Tristan replied as he continued to search the names.

They fell silent, focusing on flipping through the folders filed in the nurses' station. Periodically one or the other of them would glance at the scrap of paper to confirm the name.

After a minute or two Tristan broke the silence. "Excellent. Abigail Turner is here," he said as he pulled the file, stuffed it in his duffel and closed the bottom drawer. "Asher Wevell isn't here, but I still have Dolores and Mather to check."

"Olive, Ennis and Jeremy aren't in this drawer," Kimber replied. She closed the top drawer with a thunk. She felt surprised at none of them being present.

Tristan opened the middle drawer and they both bent to look inside.

"I still have Karol and Talone though."

They both fell silent again while they searched. It only took them another couple of minutes to scan through the remaining folders.

"I wonder why none of the rest are here?" Tristan mused. He closed the drawer. Kimber stretched out her back, faintly sore from leaning over the cabinet.

"It seems a bit unusual that so few of them have seen the nurses," she agreed. "One or two missing I might put down to chance, but all except this one? That doesn't make sense."

"Maybe they're all in the laboratory and it's chance that this woman's file is here?" Tristan suggested. Kimber nodded but she still wasn't sure.

"I can easily believe the laboratory files would all be kept separate, but if they've had a vaccine, or stitches, or anything the nurses would have kept records for, the files should still be here."

"Let's keep looking, we can think about it more later," Tristan suggested.

She followed as he led them both back into the lab, her mind still puzzling over the missing records.

Maybe Tristan's right, she thought. *Maybe the nurse's files were accumulated in the main laboratory files and we'll discover them all together.*

Then why is Abigail Turner's file in the nurse's cabinet? a small voice whispered to her.

Kimber shrugged it off. She couldn't afford to speculate. She was there to help, not make matters worse.

The laboratory was large and predominantly open-plan. One corner had been set aside for a series of workbenches and cupboards. The table was neatly ordered but filled with beakers, a small centrifuge, vortex and fume hood, pipettes, Petri dishes and piles of other regular equipment. Obviously that was where the rudimentary testing occurred.

Three gurney beds were set up along one wall, as were a number of chairs for patients or their families to sit on while waiting. Wash stations and a shelf full of disposable syringes, beakers, blood tubes and other standard paraphernalia were set up in a small area. There was plenty of space in the middle of the room— obviously most of the room being needed at a moment's notice for ambulance trolleys to pick up patients, as well as needing a general walk-way for people to move around the different stations.

"There isn't a filing cabinet," Tristan spoke. His voice sounded hollow to Kimber, deflated.

Some expert consultant you're turning out to be, the negative part of her brain decreed.

She searched the room again, hoping to find inspiration.

Chapter Five

"We need to check the rest of the facility," Tristan insisted.

"No, not yet," Kimber replied. She scanned the laboratory for a third time. The workbenches with beakers and test tubes, the gurneys, the wash station, the long table evidently used as a desk with a few neat folders in a rack of in-trays…the stickers on the row of trays finally caught her attention.

'In', 'To File' and 'To Archive'.

"There." She pointed to the desk, feeling a surge of triumph.

"To File," she added. "Maybe we'll get lucky and the reason none of our other names are in the cabinet is because they're really slow to put these things away."

Tristan followed a pace behind her as she hurried across the lab. She wasn't sure why but Kimber had the feeling that time was slipping through her fingers.

"We all clear out there, mate?" Tristan said, presumably into his comm. Kimber reached the desk and started flipping through the top tray, the one marked 'In' while Tristan tilted his head, seeming to listen to Lucas' response.

Tristan gave her some space, but came to the side of the desk she stood at, remaining in her peripheral vision. She hastily flicked through the dozen or so files. None matched her list. Mentally keeping her fingers crossed she moved onto the 'To File' tray. This one was thicker, perhaps two dozen files.

"Come on, come on," she murmured mostly under her breath as if her urging could make the files appear.

"No, we've only found one. We'll still be a good few minutes," Tristan replied to Lucas. "Let me know the minute you sniff something not right."

"Damn it all to hell," Kimber cursed as she double-checked the last name on the file. She could hardly believe her poor luck. None of the eight remaining names were there.

"What?" Tristan snapped.

Kimber turned to scorch him with a deadly look, only to see the tension and worry on his face. He glanced from her to their surroundings, his hand resting behind his back.

Kimber realised he had almost drawn his weapon at her curse. They were both on edge, but while she was feeling largely frustrated, he appeared worried about their safety. She surmised he'd thought her swearing was because they'd been caught out.

"None of them are here," she said, feeling horridly exasperated.

"Then we check the main medical files," Tristan replied and began to cross the room, heading towards the door once again.

"Hang on, I might as well check the archiving pile while I'm here," she halted him.

Tristan paused at her words, tension rippling through his stance.

Kimber took a gamble that he wouldn't leave her, looked back down and quickly rifled through the last dozen folders in the 'To Archive' pile.

As she had guessed, Tristan moved closer back to her, though still remained a few paces away. She could see the faint jiggle as he tapped his foot.

"Ha!" she cried out, pulling a folder from the pile. "I've got you, Ennis Farlough."

Flushed with her success, she placed it on the edge of the desk in easy reach and scanned even faster through the last few files.

"Holy shit!" she crowed in delight. "Here's Dolores Kienl and Mather Niese as well. What a coup."

"But the others aren't there?" Tristan said, clearly confused.

Kimber shook her head and opened Mather's file.

"I don't even understand the implications of these three being here. They're supposedly waiting to be 'archived'," she reminded him.

Any further hypothesising dropped out of mind as her brain registered what her eyes saw. Clearly stamped across the front sheet of paper — the most recent page of the file — was a single red word.

Deceased.

Kimber's eyes widened. She continued to scan the notes. Tristan came to read over her shoulder.

'10/02 – MN declared DOA, death certificate issued, cause of death: heart failure

09/02 – MN check-up, reaction OK, no further follow up – BP 120/80, BT – 36.7 °C pupils reactive – OK

07/02 – MN received third dose of vaccine I79. Mild skin reaction – OK. BP 110/80, BT – 36.5°C pupils reactive – OK
13/11 – MN check-up OK, no further follow up – BP 120/90, BT – 36.4 °C pupils reactive – OK
10/11 – MN received second dose of vaccine I79...'

Leaving Mather Niese's folder open on the desk so Tristan could continue to read it, she briefly scanned Ennis Farlough and Dolores Kienl's files as well. Both of them had passed away in the last few months and both had received numerous doses of the vaccine – I79 – mentioned in Mather's file.

The doctor's notations seemed similar in all three cases. All three of them were consulted by and signed off on by a Dr Paul Harper. Most distressing was that while each of these patients had died recently from seemingly different causes, they all had passed away mere days after having another shot of the I79.

Kimber flicked over the notation page and read the reports of the most recent blood analysis. She wasn't a doctor, but her background in vaccines and immunology helped her enough to get a rough idea of what the tests concluded. Red and white blood cell counts, platelets analysis and all kinds of tests – they were analysing these people's immune reactions, presumably to this vaccine I79.

"We have to find these other files," Kimber said urgently, her mind moving in a hundred different directions. "It appears as if Project Immunity is some sort of vaccine being tested on people. They're monitoring white blood cell counts and the levels of various Immunoglobulin. It's not supposed to be like this. Clinical trials take years and reams of paperwork, a hundred different control panels, interviews. The red tape is mind boggling. How the hell did this tiny little pseudo-laboratory get permission to—"

"Henley's using money and resources she's received illegally through back channels—" Tristan cut her off. "My guess is they didn't get permission from the various government medical boards or agencies, love."

"But..." Kimber couldn't even finish the sentence, unable to stomach such a thought. She looked wildly about her, unable to believe this innocuous room could have been privy to something so mind-numbing.

And to have potentially resulted in deaths... Kimber struggled to catch her breath. She had to be overreacting. This couldn't possibly be as it seemed.

Her gaze fell back on the test tubes. Almost blindly she focused on their colour-coded caps waiting to be pierced by needles and filled with blood. Her attention roamed towards the centrifuge and dishes in the corner, beakers lined up along the bench waiting for the laboratory staff to return for the following day.

In a rush she collected up the three folders and shoved them into Tristan's duffel. She could pore over them later, when she had time to pick them apart at leisure. For now she needed to act while she had the chance. Kimber seriously doubted they would have another opportunity to scour the lab for samples that might be left lying around.

Determined to use every second granted to her, she stalked to the work area, knelt down and threw open the cupboard doors. With more haste than grace or care she began to search the neatly stacked piles of equipment.

She could not leave without hard evidence and a means to stop this nightmare. All thoughts of capture, of arrest for the now seemingly negligible crime of breaking and entering illegally had flown out of her mind as righteous indignation took control of her.

"Kimber! What the hell are you—?"

"If they're really doing this, if this Dr Harper is injecting people with some bloody vaccine that is resulting in their deaths, then there must be evidence," she ground out as she finished with one cupboard and moved to the next without a pause. "We don't have time or the right tools to search the place for his notes and files. But there should be blood samples, smear samples or microscope slides, hell, I'd even love a vial of this so-called vaccine. Something to use as proof."

"No, Lucas, we're fine," Tristan spoke to his comm unit. "Kimber is just…uh…"

"I have not lost my mind," she insisted without even glancing at Tristan. His tone of voice spoke volumes for what he had left unsaid.

"Of course not, love," he reassured her, hastily adding, "Fuck me, Lucas. Of course I wasn't speaking to you, you arse!"

A reluctant huff of laughter escaped her lips as she stood up and nudged the cupboard doors closed with her hip. Casting a brief glance at her lover, she gave him a half-hearted smile before opening the cupboards above the workbench.

Tristan glanced around the laboratory, looking frazzled.

"This might be a stupid question," Tristan said, seeming hesitant, "but if this is a vaccine then why are they inoculated roughly every three months? Shouldn't they just be popped once and then covered for life?"

"Many vaccines don't last for long," Kimber replied without pausing in her rapid search. "Think of an allergy shot. You need to have them frequently to help build up your immunity. Some vaccines are like you say—you have one and are covered for years or even decades—but many aren't like that. Your body needs to continually be reminded of how to fight it."

"So these people might have died from an overdose?" Tristan suggested.

Kimber shrugged.

"I can't answer that at the moment. Maybe. Possibly the good doctor continued to tweak the vaccine and made a mistake. Or maybe they had an allergic reaction to something in the vaccine. There could be a hundred different explanations. That's one of the reasons I want to find a sample."

"Let me help you," Tristan said. He came up beside her.

Suddenly, she felt antsy. They were taking too long. Kimber shook her head and moved to the last cupboard.

"No, I'm nearly done here," she insisted. "Why don't you go up front and see how simple it would be to crack into the main medical records. I know we currently have enough data to hang this bastard, but I'd feel better if we had records on those other missing patients."

Tristan hovered, clearly torn.

She paused in her search and turned to face him. Cupping his jaw tenderly, she pressed a soft, heartfelt kiss to his lips. He tasted spicy from the Indian curry they'd shared earlier for dinner. It felt like a lifetime ago. Running the tip of her tongue over the fullness of his lower lip, she felt a shiver of passion race through her body at the intimate contact.

"I'll be fine, I'm a big girl," she whispered. "Besides, I just have this cupboard to look through. I'll be less than a minute, practically on your heels. Go."

"This goes against my better judgement," he hedged. "My gut thinks—"

"That's your libido, lover," she teased him lightly. "One minute. I promise. Please, you're wasting time we don't have. Go, Tristan."

He cupped the base of her skull, his fingers splayed into her curls, and he tilted her head back to kiss her fiercely. Feeling claimed, branded, it took Kimber a minute to realise he'd pulled back, heat from his possession still tingling over her lips and neck even after he'd stepped away.

"Wow," she breathed, amazed how one man could affect her on such an elemental level.

"One minute," he reminded her.

She snapped back to attention. His decadent kiss injected eagerness and a hot, liquid thrill back into her senses. Her excitement for this work rose once again. Her spirits had flagged with the serious nature of what they had unearthed, but the simple caress of his lips, the banter that had begun to feel familiar to her lifted her enthusiasm.

Once again this felt like a grand adventure—a steamy, magnificently erotic adventure.

Tristan had only just stepped out of the laboratory when she found something. Right at the back, under a section with a sticky label stating 'Dr Harper' was a plastic rack with a bunch of vials.

While most of the caps were punctured—indicating the tests had been run and the samples were no longer viable—the two up the front were still sealed. With no context, Kimberly couldn't be sure, but she felt confident the samples were still fresh and intact, indicating he had not got around to testing them yet.

One was labelled 'Elise Heckett', the other, thrillingly, had the name 'Abigail Turner' written in a neat script.

"Got it!" she called out. She grabbed Abigail's sample and carefully slid it into the front pocket of her jeans.

Three steps across the room and things happened all at once. Tristan walked back into the lab, a smile on his face, his mouth opening as he almost said something. The sound of a gun being cocked came from across the room. A strange voice called out, "What the hell?"

Kimber snapped her head around—a tall, gangly man with shaggy, wavy blond hair almost reaching his collar was stood in a doorframe half hidden by a partially drawn privacy screen. His white lab coat flapped open, revealing suit pants and a polo shirt, a stethoscope partially lodged in the breast pocket.

He pointed a gun at Kimber, but when the man noticed Tristan coming farther into the room he swung the gun around to him, clearly sensing Tristan would be the greater threat.

"Don't shoot!" Kimber cried out. "It's okay, we're just here to—"

"Steal my work! Of course! I've been waiting for people just like you to realise the greatness I'm on the brink of."

Kimber frowned, lost. *Greatness?*

Before she could think of how to reply the man closed his eyes and squeezed off a round. The gun boomed in the enclosed space, seeming to reverberate around the laboratory. Instinctively cringing back,

Kimber clapped her hands over her ears, the sound painful to her.

Tristan had ducked for cover and now had his own gun out. Dimly Kimber thought she heard him shout, "Don't make me do this!" But the other man had already depressed the trigger once again.

With no cover to speak of Kimber trembled, feeling vulnerable. On his knees, Tristan leaned from behind the desk and shot off a couple of rounds, then waved for Kimber to come towards him. Her hands shook where they were pressed up against her ears, and for a split second she hesitated.

The stranger returned one shot, the bullet lodging into the wood Tristan was hiding behind, splintering some of it off. Understanding dawned as adrenaline pumped through her body. Sooner or later the man would get around to her, and she didn't have a desk or anything more than a thin plastic chair within reach to use for cover.

While she might get shot running for safety, she would definitely get shot if she stayed there for long.

Put like that her choice was easy.

Tristan leaned out again, a trickle of blood running down his cheek. That more than anything urged her to race towards him. Dark hair fell over his forehead. He looked far grimmer than she had seen him so far. Eyes as black as night didn't move from his target and Kimber could see his focus was absolute.

Tristan took aim and fired, the gun blasting in his hands as she crouched behind him, cowering beneath his large frame like a kid playing hide-and-seek. The other man yelped in pain and fell to the floor. Kimber only wasted a half second to glance back at him. Tristan had grazed their attacker's arm, blood was seeping into his white coat a bright, frothy red.

Looking him over carefully, she realised the wound wasn't life-threatening. She wondered if he'd done that on purpose but didn't intend for either of them to stick around and talk about it.

Reaching out, she grabbed Tristan and pulled him out of the door with her.

"We should—"

"Run like fury," she cut him off, refusing to debate about it. "I have the sample, and I don't care who he is, what he's doing here or anything of that sort. I want us to get out of here and not have to explain anything to the cops."

"I was going to say go around the back and meet up with Lucas, but it's a bit late now," he replied calmly.

Kimber's heart pounded so hard she thought for sure she'd burst a blood vessel or cause some irreparable harm. She didn't understand how Tristan could be so cool about all of this. A part of her felt immense pride she wasn't having a hysterical meltdown in the middle of the waiting room as they both rushed towards the front door.

"We're fine," Tristan spoke into his comm.. "We've been compromised. I need you to call someone at the Agency and get them to remove the CCTV for this hour, immediately. We're heading out of the front and can't afford to be seen. Get the fuck out of there. We're going dark for now. I'll call you later when we're safely stashed away."

Lucas must have given his assent immediately because less than a breath later Tristan said, "Okay," before removing his ear piece and putting it in his pocket.

Remembering her key card, Kimber dug her hands into both her back pockets, struggling to remember which one she'd put it in. The clock in the waiting room told her they'd been inside the clinic for less than half an hour. She could hardly credit it and part of her brain insisted the clock must be wrong.

She felt like she'd spent half her life in those two rooms.

Tristan opened the front door.

"We're inside already, no need for the card," he said, his mind clearly on other things. With a gulp Kimber followed him outside. He clasped one large hand around her upper arm—her mind recognised the fact that despite their hasty flight and her near panic, his touch was firm but quite gentle, he didn't manhandle her or hold her overly tightly—and steered her towards the nearest Tube stop.

"We're going dark and I will need to take countermeasures to be certain we're not followed," he said. He moved his head constantly so he could watch every direction and scan the streets. "Are you hurt? Did that bastard hit you?"

"No," she gasped, her mind still reeling with all that had happened. "I'm fine. I swear."

"Will you be able to hold it together for an hour or so?" He lowered his voice as they turned onto a well-lit street. No one was in hearing distance but they were moving towards a busy street and soon would have many people around them.

Kimber took a moment to collect herself and nodded.

"Yes. Yes, I'm fine," she reassured him.

She looked up at Tristan. He gazed back at her for a second. She smiled, hoping her trust in him—and not the fear she rapidly pushed to the back of her mind—would show through.

Tristan released her and wrapped his arm around her shoulder, drawing her body closely into the curve of his own. He pressed a warm kiss to her forehead.

"You're a brave girl," he said, emotion rich in his tone. "Plenty of guts. I just want to be certain we aren't followed."

Kimber reached up a hand and wiped away the trail of blood down the side of his face.

"You need a doctor," she insisted. "Or at least get me to a first-aid kit. It's only a scratch, but it needs cleaning and maybe a bit of adhesive tape."

Tristan saw the blood on her fingers and blinked in clear surprise. He ran a hand over the thin graze, rubbed it a moment then tugged his hair to cover the worst of it.

"I can't feel a thing," he promised. "Chances are it's a splinter from that damn desk the bastard shot out. Let me know if it gets worse. Covering our tracks is more important than cleaning that up."

Kimber didn't demur, but glanced at him every few seconds to keep an eye on his wound. Two blocks later Tristan started doubling back, walking them on a convoluted, winding path up and down the city streets, constantly checking around them and in the reflections of windows to make certain they were safe. Even though her insides were still shaking with reaction and the faint tinge of fear, she had never felt more protected or safe.

Kimber knew first-hand now that adventure, romance, passion and excitement were not exactly the same as what she had seen and read about for most of her life. The thrill had a keen edge to it, a sharp bite she'd not fully understood or expected. But one thing she knew without doubt—this man—her lover and partner—would protect her with his all, until his dying breath.

She could trust him with her heart, her soul and her life.

He would protect and cherish her always.

He was her hero.

Later, she would realise this was the very moment she fell deeply, desperately and irrevocably in love with Tristan Walters.

Chapter Six

It wasn't until Kimber first dabbed the antiseptic ointment onto his brow that Tristan felt the pain of his cut. Adrenaline had always been better than any drug he'd heard of. For him, it cut through pain, fear, self-doubt and pretty much anything other than the mental clarity of what his next action could be.

In the heat of the moment adrenaline always caused his mind to be razor-sharp, perfectly clear in its focus and dull to anything else external. This time the dangerous threat to Kimber had kept his endorphin levels high. He'd lost Peterson, that pain was still quite raw and vivid in his mind.

At the time he'd not been able to do anything for his mate. Wounded, half unconscious from lack of blood and shock, his work partner being shot in the face had occurred in the space of an eye blink. The mere thought of Kimber being in danger had knotted his stomach uncomfortably. That moment when the gun had fired for the first time many things had crystallised for him.

The very certain knowledge that he loved this woman had become painfully apparent. Nothing could happen to her. Not while he still drew breath and could protect her.

Amazingly she had borne up well. He had taken them on a maze-like walk long into the early hours of the morning. Swapping trains, routes, carriages and even rising up to the streets above to check their tail by wandering the small alleys, losing any passers-by in the shops, then doubling back to repeat the process for nearly two hours had at least convinced him that they had not been tailed and their escape had been clear.

Throughout all that time Kimber had not uttered one word of protest. Any other woman—and more than a few men Tristan knew, as well—would have protested long before he had finally wound their way back to his flat. As he had put his key into the lock and had opened his front door Kimber had finally snapped out of her own thoughts. She glanced at him, seeming curious, perhaps searching his face for something.

"Is this your place?" she asked, her voice soft and husky. They'd spent most of the last hour in silence as her exhaustion and the letdown from her own adrenaline surge had almost certainly slowed her.

Tristan nodded and held her close to him while opening the door. He scanned his entryway to be certain they wouldn't be ambushed. The visible coast clear, he kissed her forehead tenderly, amazed at her resilience. She was no weeping sop, ready to fall apart at the merest hint of adversity.

"Yes, this is my home," he replied, admiration burning strongly in him. The fierce need to protect her still raged strongly. "Wait here a moment while I check out we're safe, okay?"

She nodded, leaning against his door-jamb with a tiny sigh of relief.

Tristan quickly scouted his small flat. Confident the place was secure, he returned to Kimber and paused just for a moment to stare at her and drink the sight in.

Her golden curls were mussed from their flight, spiralling adorably out of control. They made her appear like some wild pagan goddess after a fight to the death. Warm blue eyes showed tiredness, but still plenty of spirit and determination. Her dark clothes were crumpled, a small bulge in her jeans pocket reminding him they had not left empty-handed.

Tristan dropped his duffel on the small entryway table with relief then crossed the distance back to Kimber and gently led her into his home. The door closed behind them and he checked the locks were secure before taking her hand and urging her into his main living room.

He was about to sit her on the couch and offer to make her some tea to soothe her nerves, but she took him by surprise again. Her hair fell to her shoulders when she tilted her head at him.

"Where's that first-aid kit of yours?" she asked, strength returning to her voice, the tiredness evidently pushed back once again. Worry spiked through him.

"You said you weren't hurt," he insisted. Sitting beside her, squashing her unceremoniously to one corner of the large padded chair, he ran a hand professionally down her arm, searching for wounds which after all this time would need immediate care.

She chuckled, her slender hands gentle as she cupped his jaw and lifted his face to meet hers.

"Not for me, lover," she chided him. She brushed the tip of her finger, whisper-light, over the corner of his brow, coming away with a tiny amount of dried blood.

"Oh," he replied, chagrined to have forgotten the small scratch. "It's nothing. We should shower and call in, check Lucas made it all right and managed to get those cameras wiped. Then—"

"I followed you without question for two hours." She tapped his nose smartly, her tone brooking no argument. "You can give me five minutes to assuage my worry and clean that wound. Then you can get back to saving the world once again, I swear."

He grinned, unable to resist her taking charge. It heated his blood, fired him up and made his cock twitch with eagerness. She was far braver than she realised, he knew—more courageous than he could have possibly guessed from her petite frame, her sensual curls or her brainy manner.

A few minutes would not change anything.

He nodded and stood, waving a hand towards the bathroom.

"Back here," he said.

She followed him once again. Sitting on the edge of the bath, he waited while she sorted through his large tub of medical paraphernalia, picking and choosing what she wanted to use.

When she dabbed the ointment onto his graze, he hissed briefly at the completely unexpected pain. She huffed in barely suppressed laughter once then swallowed her amusement.

"You sure know how to show a girl a good time," she spoke after a moment. The let-down after a death-defying experience always affected people differently, Tristan knew from long experience.

"I've had my fair share of complaints from women," he replied, feeling his way through what she was getting at.

"I can't think why. We achieved part of what we set out to do, you protected me, would have clearly given your life to keep me safe. Then you got us out of there and made certain we were no longer in danger. I wasn't being facetious. It wasn't quite how I planned to end out first criminal act together, but all up I think you did a marvellous job."

Tristan chuckled dryly.

"Sure, this time I only got grazed. Last time I was shot it took months—" His words cut off at the painful memory. Soft lips pressed to his. Tristan's inner musing halted immediately. Kimber's touch, her taste and faint, sweet scent took all the horrible memories away in an instant.

He stroked his tongue out over her lips, tasting her. He craved experiencing her even more intimately and wondered what her juices would be like rolling around in his mouth when it was just her natural flavours, with no hint of his own salty skin. She pulled away and he sighed at the loss.

"We're both completely safe and here because of you," she reminded him as she dabbed more ointment on his wound. "You might have taken us on the long route back, but we're here and fine. Now let me tend to you and then we can call in or report or do whatever you need."

The fact she could joke and poke fun at him settled matters in his mind. She was fine, coping far better than he could have imagined. The pale, fearful look that had been on her face in the laboratory was long gone and she had bounced back stronger and sassier than ever.

Heat filled his body and he tried to put a lid on it. Sexual urgency was another common side effect of action they'd been through. It had never been so potent, so overwhelmingly needy, but he tried to get himself under control nevertheless.

When she leaned over, studying his cut, her light, floral scent consumed his senses. He discreetly breathed her in, holding the feminine nature of her smell within his body and committing it to memory.

Tristan had learnt long ago he was not the sort of man women wanted to build a life with—gone at all hours, sometimes for days or even weeks at a time. Secretive about the nature of his work, unable to share much of the burden he frequently carried inside him, and then coming home battered, bruised and bloody.

Yeah, some catch I am.

His disastrous relationship track record aside, Tristan knew deep in his soul that Kimber was different. She was special. He planned to cling to her acceptance, desire and warmth for as long as she chose to stay. She would leave sooner or later, fed up with him, every woman had so far, but for now, he planned to relish every moment, every caress and everything she gave him so willingly. The look in her eyes as she tended to him was so loving, so tender, he could almost convince himself he'd finally found a woman who could accept all of him unconditionally and still care for the man he tried so hard to be.

She tenderly pressed the adhesive tape over his cut, brushing his hair back out from his eyes as she did so. They both paused, each seeming reluctant for this perfect moment to end. She stared at him, and for the first time in what felt like forever he wished he could read minds and understand women better.

"What?" he asked in a low tone, a small smile tilting the corners of his mouth. His body hummed with desire, blood surging into his cock and stiffening him. He knew the faintest touch or gesture of acceptance would set him over the edge. Tristan could feel himself poised, ready to take her over and over, claim her as his.

In truth he had no idea if this was lasting love or just the culmination of a heady mixture of a beautiful woman, hormones and an intoxicating situation. It felt real to him, the desires and urges he felt towards Kimber were not fleeting or passing, were not weak, easily shattered feelings. He wanted her more than anything else in this world, and he knew that would not change when she woke up the following morning and realised exactly what she had got herself into.

"I just..." Kimber's voice trailed off and she shook her head. She straddled his lap and sat down, the heat of her pussy penetrating his hard cock. He felt her need through their denims. Sensing the urgency in her touch and seeing the fine tremors that shivered along her fingers, he knew how much she craved this.

When she kissed him fire raged through his body, burning away every doubt and question he could possibly hold. Any pretence at restraint evaporated and he kissed her back. Swiftly, he moved a hand up to cup her head and tilt it. This way he could plunge his tongue deeply inside her mouth. Soft curls fell over his skin, taunting him and driving his lust higher.

Tristan moaned with the fierce passion of his need. He could not have restrained himself even if every soldier from Hades had stormed into his bathroom. Kimber cried out passionately, her legs wrapped around his waist and they pressed against each other. Tristan thrust his cock against her, simulating their ardent lovemaking even through their clothes. She whimpered, arching into him desperately at his movement

Holding her legs high, he stood, then carefully lowered her to the cool tile floor. Kissing each other as if the world was about to end, they stripped each other naked with far more haste than grace. The thin lace of her bra and knickers tore at his rough tugging, their clothes scattered wherever they fell.

Finally they were both naked and he could look his fill at her curvy, tiny body.

She was perfect, everything he could possibly want or imagine. And for now at least, she was his, this beautiful, passionate woman he had fallen irrevocably in love with.

Kimber didn't feel any of the usual shyness or embarrassment of having a man look at her naked body. Splayed like some ancient offering—open and totally accessible to him on his bathroom floor—had someone told her two days ago she'd be in this position, ravenous for a man she had known for less than twenty-four hours, she'd have laughed at the joke.

Far from some shy virgin, or self-conscious spinster, Kimber enjoyed her body and her sexual satisfaction, but that didn't mean she paraded around naked, or prostrated herself in front of random strangers and asked coyly if they liked what they saw.

Tristan, however, was no random stranger. They knew things about each other, integral, elemental parts of each other's psyche and true selves.

Besides, the heat and sensual awareness in the man's dark gaze, the way his eyes devoured her like some delicious treat could not go unanswered. She craved this man, loved him deeply. She wanted him more than she could possibly ever put into words or explain to another.

Arching up, she cupped his face, brought him down to cover her body and kissed him like a starving woman. She slid her hands down the curve of his spine, palmed his arse and drew him intimately close, so his cock nudged at her entrance. She wanted to feel him, every hot, decadent inch of his cock, then feel his seed splash inside her body.

"I'm safe," she whispered in his ear, hoping he knew her meaning.

"Me too, tested regularly," he replied huskily. He held her hip with one of his large hands, pausing as if waiting for permission to enter her fully.

"Fuck me, Tristan, please, I need to have you, all of you."

Moaning when their lips met once again, he pierced her core in a single, sensual thrust. Stretched unbearably tight, Kimber arched up, panting. She struggled to encompass his thick length. Their eyes met and in the silence only their ragged breaths could be heard.

Kimber felt as if she were looking into her lover's very soul. She relaxed her muscles around his cock and her body turned liquid, the heat of her desire easing his passage.

Rocking into her, Tristan thrust with a series of lazy, sensual movements, slowly gathering momentum as he penetrated her deeper each time. Without a word they continued to stare at each other.

Each thrust rippled through her senses, driving her passions higher. Her face flushed with the heat of her sexual excitement, tiny beads of sweat making her skin slick from lust. Regardless, she couldn't break the perfection of this moment. She lost herself in his eyes. A part of her felt as if they were opening themselves emotionally and spiritually as they watched each other, noting every move, every twitch, every aspect of their lovemaking. It was easily the most intimate, soul-baring moment of her life, and she felt overjoyed to be sharing such a deep, elemental part of herself with this man.

I love you. The words reverberated silently in her head. Kimber longed to share this part of her feelings with him — but she feared it would be too much, too soon. She didn't want to freak him out, or chase him away by asking for more than he was willing to give.

Her imagination, always overactive, could easily picture him whispering the same words to her as they came together in this union of souls.

"Fuck but you're beautiful," Tristan murmured. He roved his gaze over her face, seeming to take her all in and memorise her.

Kimber grinned and reached her hands around to grab his arse and drag him closer so they were pressed flush against each other.

"You're a bloody handsome man yourself," she replied, meaning every word.

They kissed again, the delicate spell between them shattering in the heat of their need for one another.

Kimber lifted to meet Tristan's thrusts, crying out as he dipped his head and his mouth encompassed one of her nipples. The suckling sent small jolts through her body, her pleasure spiking. Her grip over the building orgasm slipped and she could feel her peak nearing.

"Mmm," he murmured. He fondled her breast for a moment, then lightly pinched her other nipple. His teeth rasping over the sensitive nub sent her spiralling out of control. Wanting him with her every step of the way, Kimber clenched her inner muscles down tightly on his pulsing shaft, squeezing him in the most intimate of caresses.

"Fuck!" he cried out.

She watched his eyes widen and a tremor shake his body. Piercing her with rapid, hard strokes now, he rode through her climax, his own seeming to take him by surprise.

Heat splashed inside her as his seed shot into her womb. Short, sharp thrusts filled her to breaking point and Kimber screamed. She shook uncontrollably, caught up in the momentum of her orgasm. They scrabbled to pull one another closer, locked together in the most intimate of embraces.

Slowly she fell back to earth, panting, and slid against the tiled floor as sweat coated her skin. Gasping, it took them both a moment to gather their breath. Kimber threaded her hands tenderly through Tristan's hair, enjoying the soft feel against her hot skin.

"See?" she teased, "I told you—you know how to show a girl a good time."

"Any time," he replied, his words joking but the look in his eyes serious. "For you, love, I'm willing any time."

Satisfied beyond her wildest dreams, Kimber grinned as he wrapped her up in his warm embrace.

* * * *

"I need to get into the laboratory at work," Kimber said while she finger-combed her damp hair into what she hoped would be a semblance of order. Steam filled

Tristan's small bathroom so the mirror was practically useless to tell just how much of a mess she looked.

Tristan had suggested they'd shower. When she'd admitted she hadn't wanted to move, he'd confessed to similar thoughts. Logic had had her facing reality though. Together they'd shared a hot, indulgent shower full of laughter and playfulness. Despite the lateness of the hour — or earliness, depending on how you looked at it — she was now bursting with energy. Kimber could only surmise it had come from the danger of their situation. Normally at three in the morning she was sound asleep.

"I need to let Lucas know we're all right first," Tristan groaned. Her words seemed to penetrate his mind then. "That sample you took, you can run tests on it?"

"I can run a few preliminary tests," she warned him, "but with the right equipment I can run many of the more detailed ones. I don't work in immunology at the moment, so work doesn't have all the instruments I'd need."

"What if I could get you access to a lab that did? Could you do it?"

"DNA profiling and some of those tests take hours to condition," she answered cautiously. "But effectively, yes, I could get us a lot of data before breakfast."

"You're perfect," Tristan said as he planted a quick kiss on her lips.

Kimber chuckled when he moved away. She reached out, took his shoulder and pulled him back for a slower, far more thorough kiss. This time they both pulled away noticeably more sated.

"That's better," she murmured. "Go on, make your calls. Are you sure Lucas will still be up? It's an unearthly hour of the morning."

"He will," Tristan replied, then he paused. "Well, I would still be. We've only been partners a matter of months so we're still getting used to each other. I'll be surprised if he isn't pacing somewhere, waiting for my call to know we're safe."

Kimber grinned at him and pulled her hair back into a ponytail. He took his mobile phone out of his pocket and walked into the hallway. Recalling the files in his duffel, she retraced their steps back to where he had placed the bag. She opened the bag and rummaged around in it, pulling the four files out. She carried them over to the large table and spread them out.

"Hey mate, did you miss me?" Tristan spoke into his phone, his voice getting louder as he followed her into the room.

Kimber glanced up, exchanged a smile with him, then returned to her work as he sat on one edge of the couch.

Lining the folders up, she compared them against each other. She listened with half an ear to Tristan's side of their conversation and tried to piece together what seemed to be going on. The matching names made her almost positive these were a selection of the patients Henley had listed as involved in Project Immunity. The fact they were being injected with a vaccine also supported this notion.

What she couldn't understand as yet was whether Ennis, Delores and Mather's deaths were due to coincidence—surely a stretch?—or related somehow to the vaccine.

Checking the dates against the notations, she knew they were all being inoculated roughly every three months, which she knew was about how regularly the body replenished its white blood cells. Flipping to the last page, she noticed none of them had had their first visit in the same time period, they all had come from different areas of Greater London, nothing immediately jumped out at Kimber to explain why these people had been chosen.

"...and then this weird science freak came from nowhere—there must have been an office or something out back we missed—and lost his mind. Started shooting at us...yeah I know, we weren't being angels there, but that's no reason to open fire on us..."

Starting at the beginning, she discovered that of the four patients, Ennis was injected first almost twelve months ago. Interestingly, she noted he'd been injected with I78, not I79. She looked about her for pen and paper. Kimber grabbed an empty envelope, then crossed back to the duffel. Rummaging through it she found a pen in a small zippered compartment.

Sitting back down, she made the notation to check I78 vs I79 and follow up whether it was actually a newer version of the vaccine.

Ennis had been inoculated twice, then two months later both Mather and Dolores had started within a week of each other. Six weeks after that Abigail had also been vaccinated for the first time.

Hoping that to see the timeline laid out sequentially would help, Kimber printed it all out in small letters, noting the dates of each vaccination. With luck, there'd be a pattern. Aside from the regularity of the shots, nothing struck her as interesting.

"...yeah, I know, Morrison cracks the shits when he gets woken up in the middle of the night...hell yeah, I've heard that story. I was there when Campos found the bones in his top desk drawer. Never heard an agent scream so shrilly."

Distracted, Kimber lifted her head and caught Tristan's gaze. He snickered and moved his phone away for a second.

"Morrison is our main medical," he explained hastily. "Excellent man, but can be a cranky sonofabitch sometimes. Practical joker too. Glued a hand into the base of a mate's desk drawer—every single bone in exact place—and scared the shit out of him. Morrison doesn't like to be called out in the middle of the night unless it's real important. Guy has a wife and five daughters, figures he deserves to have a semblance of a life and I can't blame him."

"Ah, thanks," Kimber laughed.

"So who else can we call at this hour?" Tristan spoke back into his phone. "I can probably call in a few favours to get use of a lab, but I'd like to hold onto the only markers I have in that area. Surely you've got some chick you can call to sweet-talk, maybe take out for a nice dinner when this is done…"

Tuning out the ribald teasing between the two men, Kimber set back to work. She made a note of Abigail's phone number and address, wondering if they should be a lot more worried that this young woman appeared to be the only patient still alive. Was it significant? Kimber wished she had more answers.

Studying Abigail's file thoroughly, she tried to will her tired brain to make some giant leap forward and discover something brilliant.

Twenty-nine years old, five-foot-six and seeming in good health, the woman did not spark any miraculous understanding in Kimber. She'd been in for her check-up the previous day—which likely explained the blood vial Kimber had found stashed away awaiting testing—but the brief, clinical notes were not revealing.

Wishing she had this Dr Harper's private notes, which almost certainly would be far more forthcoming, Kimber reviewed the files one last time.

"Lucas is going to call us back in a minute," Tristan's voice came from right beside her.

Kimber jumped slightly—still edgy from the mental weight of the files and what they symbolised. She sighed and leaned her head against the flat planes of Tristan's stomach. She tried to soak in his calmness, needing his strength as she tried to not overanalyse the consequences of what they had discovered so far.

"Dr Harper appears to be modifying the vaccine," she hypothesised. "I found a reference from months ago to I78. The recent entries all indicate they're using I79. This isn't some small-time back-yard deal. This is a grassroots, serious experiment. Abigail was in only yesterday for her standard check-up. That must be why I found her blood sample, Harper mustn't have got around to it yet."

Tristan rubbed her shoulders but remained silent.

Kimber closed her eyes for a moment, relishing not just at her lover's touch, but at the slow release of the tension in her muscles. He knew exactly what she needed, and she loved him all the more for that.

"Oh," she murmured, her voice thick as she tried to relax and let her worry seep out of her. "I've jotted down her number and address. I'm not sure we should call her at this horrid hour, but I'm hoping if we can talk to her without scaring her witless she might be able to fit in some of the pieces. I can't see the big picture here, and there's so many gaps and uncertainties I might go mad trying to second guess this all."

"Tomorrow morning Preston will probably insist on calling the good doctor onto the carpet and close this whole mess down," Tristan informed her.

Kimber felt a lot of the burden she'd been carrying lift. Of course, how stupid of her to not realise that.

"Preston will need to use caution," she said thoughtfully. "Abigail still has whatever this vaccine is inside her system. We'll need Harper to explain exactly what it is, or at least hand over his notes. I can tell you no scientist willingly opens their private notebooks unless they have great incentive. I can learn a lot from the tests we can run, but it will be far simpler to have Harper on our side and explain it all to us. It will go much easier for Abigail too."

"We're trained how to be…persuasive. Don't worry about it."

Kimber chuckled. Despite the wonderful feel of Tristan's fingers on her shoulders she could not relax. With a sigh tilted her head back to look at Tristan.

"I can't stop thinking about her," she confessed. "Could you call Abigail? Make up some excuse? Maybe pretend to be a wrong number, or some poor telemarketer schmuck in a different country and calculating the time zone wrong. It's gnawing at me and I can't understand why."

"Feminine instinct," Tristan murmured. He picked up his phone with one hand, still massaging her with his other as he glanced at her envelope and dialled the number she had written down. "Never let it be said I didn't trust or fully believe in the power of female intuition."

"And now you've said that Abigail will be perfectly fine and I'll be relegated to nothing more than a worry wart." Kimber chuckled.

She let her eyes close once again, confident she'd be proved a fool in a minute. Maybe the stress of the entire situation had got to her finally? She'd built something small and well-meaning into a giant turmoil inside her head. Perhaps she and Tristan could even go to bed for the few hours remaining of the night. They could get some rest, maybe sleep for a bit and then explore each other anew before starting the day once more.

She'd love to run her tongue all over his cock, suck him down while stroking his balls. She bet he'd —

"Oh shit," Tristan said. His hand moved from her shoulder and Kimber felt a sinking in her stomach. She looked up at him and watched him redial the number, his features taut with strain.

She knew something was wrong, anyone could see that.

Tristan held the phone pressed to his ear for a moment, shaking his head angrily as he hung up again.

"Her line is disconnected. There's no answer."

The brief moment of self-doubt evaporated and all of Kimber's earlier worries crowded back into her mind. She'd known it couldn't have been that simple after all.

Chapter Seven

It wasn't often Tristan felt completely out of his depth.

He knew his strengths and weaknesses. Tristan was a smart man. Used to action and making decisions based on scraps of knowledge and far too little time, he had an enviable success rate on completing his missions. The years had given him an instinctive understanding of when to ask for help, when to slog it out himself and when to just shoot or burn everything in sight.

Until recently he had felt there was very little he couldn't overcome or succeed in.

In a short space of time, however, he had lost his partner, discovered his boss had hoodwinked their entire division and fallen in love with the brainiest lady scientist it had ever been his pleasure to know.

Watching Kimber move around the laboratory was a pleasure. He followed her as she used the various pieces of equipment the way a pianist would caress the keys to create beautiful music. Seeing her so obviously in her element — and far outside his meagre scientific understanding — Tristan had needed to step back and accept the fact this was her world and within these confines she ran the show.

He might be in charge while they picked locks, dodged bullets and broke multiple laws, but there in the laboratory it was Kimberly who knew what to do and how to achieve their best outcome. Tristan actually found himself relaxing while he watched Kimber work. Her movements had an easy grace to them — her familiarity with the various pieces of equipment clearly visible.

"I've decided to start with some of the most basic diagnostic tests," she said, though she continued to work. "It's been a while since I've done much of this, years, actually. I want to refresh myself and get back into the university mindset before I try some of the more complicated experiments. We only have the one sample and I don't want to mess it up."

"You heard me call Lucas earlier, he's in with some of our best hackers, trying to track down Abigail," Tristan said. "When we find her we can always ask for a blood sample if you need more."

"It might become moot if she can explain what Harper and Henley have been trying to do," Kimber agreed. She used a pipette to place a single drop of blood precisely on a glass slide. Tristan watched as she put a smaller square over the drop of blood and the capillary action caused the tiny dot to spread in a wide, see-through thin layer beneath the glass.

She appeared to juggle multiple tests at a time. Leaving the glass slides, she then placed the test tube full of blood on a fast-moving instrument which buzzed. She pressed the plastic against its side.

"This is a vortex," she explained. Tristan figured his confusion or curiosity — or possibly both — must have been visible on his face. "The mechanics are simple. This section spins around fast, and you gently press something against it. The purpose is to mix it up, to homogenise the sample and make certain the tiny amount you take to test is representative of the whole tube."

Tristan chuckled and nodded, the answer surprisingly simple for what at a first glance had appeared to be a complex thing.

"Seeing as I have pierced the seal I plan to set up as many tests as I can perform," she continued. "I will reseal the tube when I'm done, but blood oxidises very quickly. I can't swear that placing a new cap on the tube will keep it from decaying. This is very much in for a penny, in for a pound. I can only do my best."

"It'll be fine," Tristan reassured her. "I can tell you've already set up a number of tests, even if they simply rule out things Henley and Harper are doing, it will all assist us. I trust you."

Kimber threw him a harried but brilliantly bright smile, then she gathered fresh pipettes and continued to work.

"I'm setting up some gels and doing some loop streaks to see what kinds of cultures I can grow with the sample. I also want to do some stains and smears, maybe even run a few chromatographs. These are all regular diagnostics and from that I can move forward on hopefully some more complex tests that will narrow down the field."

"More complex tests?" Tristan echoed.

Kimber laughed.

"Have I told you that I've never shot a gun before?"

The statement struck Tristan as a strange thing for her to confess right now.

"When we were in the clinic, and you were shooting at that worker, I felt completely out of my depth. Even though I've always wanted to do something like this, I realised we all have our own areas of expertise. This here, now, is mine. But that doesn't make you or your skills any less impressive."

Tristan grinned, touched that she was sensitive enough to say something so kind to him. She had a soft heart, his Kimber.

"How about I teach you how to shoot?" he offered. "I can help you practice, and next time we're in a similar situation you can shoot the bad guys and I can boast arrogantly about how magnificent you are?"

Kimber laughed and dropped purple liquid onto the microscope slide. The red drop of blood instantly turned a dark black/purple. She picked the glass up and walked to place it under a microscope.

"There will be a next time?" she teased him.

"Good point. If I have my way you'll never be in a situation like that again. But the offer of shooting lessons still stands."

Kimber studied him intently. Again, he wished he could read her mind.

"I'd like that," she replied in a soft voice. "I'd like to spend a lot more time with you, Tristan, with or without the shooting lessons."

He wished he could take her in his arms, hold her close and never let her go, but he knew this wasn't the right time or place for that sort of affection and intimacy.

"I plan to stick with you forever, love," he answered. "If you'll let me I won't ever let you go. That's a promise."

Kimber's face lit up, her eyes warmly sparkling and her grin infectious. She nodded her head, her blonde curls bouncing. "I might just hold you to that, Agency man," she replied, then turned to lower her face and stare into the eye-piece of the microscope.

Tristan remained silent while she fiddled with the knobs, moving the slide this way and that under the lamp as she seemed to search through the tiny drop of blood. Not wanting to divert her attention or interrupt, he watched her, entranced, as she worked.

A timer she had clipped to the edge of her sweater earlier buzzed. Muttering to herself, Kimber lifted her gaze and crossed to the centrifuge. She removed the samples then walked to a fume hood. She began to dispense the separated serums out into different gel plates.

Tristan tried to follow what she was doing, but it all became too complicated for him.

The long evening began to catch up with him and he realised he had an urgent need for a hot, strong cup of tea. His instant reaction was to stay by Kimber's side, but he quashed this. She was perfectly safe there. The lab was secure and he'd only be down the hall. The shooting earlier must have rattled him far more than he had believed.

"I feel like some tea," he said, breaking Kimber's focus. "Would you like some?"

"Oh, I'd love some," she replied with enthusiasm. "I take it black and as strong as you can make it without letting it cool too much, please."

She blew him a kiss, making him chuckle.

"I might be a quarter of an hour," he warned her.

She waved a hand to indicate she'd heard him, her attention already riveted back upon her work.

"I'm not going anywhere." Her response seemed automatic, as if her mouth spoke without her brain being fully cognisant of it. "These gels will need half an hour to acclimatise before I can start adding the enzymes for digestion. And I need to centrifuge more platelets for the — wait, I'm sure you're not fussed. It will be at least an hour before I have any information even remotely interesting to share with you. I'd love to have you here watching me, but honestly, take your time."

Visions of a lovely mug of tea and perhaps a muffin or two filling his mind, Tristan left Kimber in the lab, secure in the knowledge she was right at home.

* * * *

"I want to state again these are just my preliminary findings and — far more importantly — they're just my thoughts and ideas. I don't want any of you taking them as gospel carved in stone," Kimber reiterated for the third time in as many minutes.

"Kimberly, we are fully apprised of that, but we need some theories to work on," Preston replied.

For a moment she felt envy at her friend's crisp, clean countenance. His suit was pressed to perfection, every crease sharp as a knife. His face seemed careworn but well rested. Preston ran a hand through his short black hair and glanced at her with ill-concealed impatience.

She threw a glance at Tristan, seeking his support without even consciously thinking about it. Tiredness ebbed at her body and mind, sapping her strength and making her temper short. Kimber felt rumpled, stained and on edge. She knew without even checking that she appeared even messier than she felt.

Tristan still looked like a cool drink of water. His hair was mussed, but in that sexy way, like he'd just rolled out of bed. The dark strands spiked around his face, his warm brown eyes showing only a hint of the exhaustion he must have been feeling. Lucas, on the other hand, seemed as if he had rested. Energised, he had been hassling the technology geeks into hastening their search for Abigail Turner.

Lucas, Kimber had come to realise, enjoyed the action and hectic pace of being an agent. Despite the fact the last day and a half had been everything and far more than she could have ever imagined, Kimber knew the moment she came near a comfortable, safe bed that she would happily crash and sleep for a good eight hours.

Tristan turned and caught her gaze. Their eyes locked and her heartbeat sped up.

On the other hand, if Tristan happened to be in that bed with her, she would jump his bones without a second thought. Sleep be damned. He set a fire in her knickers, no question about it. Kimber had a lifetime worth of fantasies, erotic and kinky, to live out. Tristan was exactly the sort of man with whom she wanted to enact each and every one of them out on.

Preston cleared his throat, dragging her flagging attention back to him. He raised one black eyebrow at her. With a blush she realised she'd been daydreaming, staring at Tristan, and the small office had fallen silent, waiting for her to give them the summary she'd promised.

"Right," she replied hastily, almost swallowing around her words to get them out. "I found an astonishing number of viruses in Abigail's blood, far more than I would have expected in any ordinary person. That's one of the main reasons it took me so long to get a proper handle on what I think is happening."

"So this Abigail Turner is an incredibly sick young woman?" Preston interjected.

Kimber frowned, paused before she answered. After a moment's thought she shook her head. "Not exactly," she hedged. "You see, the levels of each pathogen were incredibly low. At first I thought it was contamination of some sort, but eventually I realised many of these were low because Abigail's immune system had overcome the diseases. For a period of time after we conquer any sickness there are still traces of it in our blood."

"So she has been very sick recently?" Lucas summarised.

Again Kimber shook her head. "Not naturally, no." She winced at the uncertainty in her tone. Her audience of three stared at her. The weight of their combined curiosity made her very faintly nervous. She cleared her throat and with a final glance at Tristan took the plunge. "I think Dr Harper added multiple variants of different diseases into his vaccine. This is all pure conjecture at this point, but I think my results are leaning towards the vaccine being used not only to heighten the patient's immune response, but also to widen the spectrum of what would be natural in humans."

All three gentlemen continued to stare at her with various levels of concentration on their faces. They all remained silent and she tried to reword herself better, more concisely. "Some vaccines are very simple," she explained. "They are to help your body fight one strain of one disease. Others are more complex, like, say, the flu vaccine. They are made up of multiple different strains of the same disease to give your immune system a broad-spectrum understanding of the disease, so if the germs mutate slightly you can still recognise it correctly and fight it easily."

The men nodded their following of this logic.

"I think the reason so many different pathogens fill Abigail's blood is because in a very short space of time she has been exposed to multiple different diseases all in the one hit. The vaccine is supposed to enhance her immune response so that she can fight off all of them simultaneously. Harper, I believe, is trying to effectively make a vaccine to give humans a super immune system, possibly to rid us of sickness altogether."

"And he's doing this by using humans as guinea pigs and possibly killing them in the process?" Preston added.

Kimber shrugged, helpless to answer such a question. "It's possible the others died from coincidence, or genuinely would have died at that time regardless of any vaccine testing. It's impossible to say. We don't even know at this stage if the nine people were even aware of what was occurring, let alone a willing party to it. All I can say is that it's possible overloading their systems in such a manner led to their deaths, but it's equally possible the two things are not connected."

"Could Abigail have died in the last day or two, since she saw Dr Harper and he gave her blood test?" Tristan asked.

Lucas shook his head and interjected, "No, the first thing I had the guys check out was the local morgues and the recent death certificates. Abigail Turner has not officially died in the last three days and none of the half-dozen Jane Does who have turned up match the description we have from her medical file."

"Well, that's something at least," Preston replied. "I'm going to put top priority on finding Abigail Turner. What happens to her after she's found we can figure out when we've spoken to her. For now I want her found—preferably safe, alive and in perfect health."

"I'm already on the guys," Lucas said. "They're monitoring her cards, going through her records to find any alternate housing or boyfriends—"

"You might want to try other medical facilities, maybe respite clinics or sanatoriums," Kimber suggested.

Lucas' head swivelled to glance at her, his expression unreadable. "What? What are you saying, Kimber?" he snapped.

"Hey!" Tristan retorted sharply.

"Well, she can't just say shit like that and—"

"She's worked her arse off on this case and given us every lead we've—"

"That doesn't means she can—"

"Okay, hey!" she shouted over the two men, her anger boiling. "I'm bloody well standing right here and am not some little kid you can argue about in front of as if I don't have my own damn voice."

Both men fell silent, though Kimber felt certain it was more from surprise at the tone of her voice and acid in her words than the fact they actually had cooled down one iota. Taking what she could get, she rushed on before they could start up again. "Tristan, I love you, but in this case I'm happy to support my suggestion. Lucas, before you jump down my throat next time, maybe let me explain myself, all right?"

She paused for a moment. Looking at Tristan, she saw him visibly relax. Something inside her unclenched, glad they wouldn't argue about this later on in private. Turning to glance at Lucas, she caught his nod for her to continue, appearing suitably chastised.

"With everything Abigail has been through recently, it stands to reason that sooner or later when she's feeling unwell and decides to see a doctor she will go for a second opinion," Kimber pointed out. "I presume your people are calling Abigail's friends and family, people whom she might seek shelter or comfort from. She also very well would seek an alternative medical opinion. It's quite possible she doesn't understand why she's constantly feeling sick or even just under the weather and tired. With this vaccine bombarding her immune system it could easily make her lethargic constantly. A logical step would be to seek a second opinion. That would show on her NHS records."

"You're right," Lucas said. "Kimber, I'm sorry. I'm just a bit worked up over this. Harper and Henley taking advantage of these people, using them like lab rats...it's got under my skin a bit."

"That's fine, Lucas. I understand," she replied.

Before she could say more Preston cut in, "Get yourself sorted out, Sloan, don't make me reassign you."

Lucas nodded, his jaw set in determination. His blue gaze was troubled, but she could see from the way he'd narrowed his eyes to focus intently on something that he wasn't a man to be easily swayed.

"Right, Kimber, I need you to write your findings up in a report. Add in all the trimmings, attach the test results and detailed hypothesis with support. Also a summary of the tests you've run so I can have our own techs go over it and use it for reference later. Can you have it on my desk by close of business tonight?"

Kimber winced but nodded.

"Excellent," Preston continued. "Lucas, Tristan, I want you both to go home for at least four hours of downtime. Yes, Sloan, no arguments. You both need to decompress and catch a few hours' rest before we start up again later this afternoon. We now have a good understanding of what Henley was doing and the net is closing around Dr Harper. Let others deal with it for a few hours and come back refreshed."

At first Kimber thought Lucas might argue, but he remained silent.

Preston waited, giving each man a chance to argue their case, but nodded with satisfaction when they both remained silent.

"I want a joint report from you both outlining every step you've each taken in the last twenty-four hours, the powers that be will want a thorough timeline. If either of you have suggestions on how to move forward that will be the medium to best take it up. For now, I want to congratulate you both on an excellent job. It might not be over, but the most pressing questions have answers and we have a definite course of future action to follow up on. Be proud of what you've accomplished. Kimber, I include you in that. You've been an invaluable asset and I'm grateful for the assistance you've given us."

"Oh, I've enjoyed it," Kimber replied, surprised to be included in Preston's speech. "But that's not it for me, right? I'll come back with Tristan later this afternoon. There's still tests to be run and—"

"We'll still need your assistance, absolutely," Preston reassured her. "If you feel you need more rest, however, I want you to come in later. These guys are used to going a few days on not much sleep. I don't want you burning out, or worse, making a simple error and leading us unknowingly down the wrong path. I need you sharp and aware. Come back here only in top form, am I making myself clear?"

"Crystal," she replied with a firm nod.

"Okay, that's it, any questions?"

Kimber shook her head. Lucas stood, clearly itching to get moving. Tristan rose slower, turning towards her with a small smile. Feeling as if she shared a secret with him, she got to her feet. The three of them left Preston's office, Tristan holding the door open for her.

Lucas stalked a few paces ahead, but Tristan called to him. "Hey!"

She followed Tristan to catch up with Lucas.

"What the fuck, mate?" Tristan asked.

Lucas shrugged and wouldn't meet their eyes.

"I can't get over what's been done to this chick. I can't explain it better than that. It's staying with me. I need to resolve it," Lucas explained disjointedly.

"Bloody oath you'd better work through it. If you speak like that again about Kimber I'll—"

"I really am sorry, Kimber," Lucas apologised.

Kimber could see the sincerity in his gaze, his words heartfelt. She waved a hand, dismissing it like old news.

"Forget it, honestly. Get some rest, Lucas. You'll feel much better for it and hopefully this won't be quite so emotional or overwhelming for you. We all react strangely when we're overtired."

"I just want to check with the computer guys," he insisted. "They might have found Abigail and besides, I want to put them onto that suggestion you made about her NHS file and look into other medical facilities. With luck they'll stumble on something quickly and I can come back and we can get moving. I hate waiting around. Inaction drives me mental."

"Well, make sure you get that downtime," she urged, hoping he would heed Preston and her suggestion.

Lucas nodded but didn't actually agree. He glanced at Tristan. The two men looked at each other for a moment, then both nodded.

"We good?" Lucas asked.

Tristan nodded again.

"We're good. Go rest."

A tiny smile hitched the corner of his mouth and Lucas shook hands with his partner. Without another word he turned and left.

Kimber sighed, faintly worried for the man.

"Do you think he'll be okay?"

"Sure he will. These things are really hard sometimes when you're just getting started."

She nodded, not quite convinced but unsure why she felt so concerned. Tristan wrapped an arm around her shoulders and eagerly she turned into his embrace. They hugged for a long moment, drawing strength from one another. She took these precious few seconds to breathe in his spicy, masculine scent. Tiredness almost overwhelmed her.

"Did you mean what you said earlier?" he whispered against the curve of her neck. She frowned, her frazzled mind at a loss as to what he was referring to.

"When?"

"When you said you loved me. Did you mean it or was it just a figure of speech?"

Her heart skipped a beat, worried she might have already driven him off without meaning to.

"Oh," she replied, desperately seeking a clever thing to say but unable to come up with anything. Finally she settled on the plain, honest truth.

"Yes. Yes, I meant it, but please don't get turned off. I didn't meant to say it so soon, I don't want to scare you and—"

"I love you too," he cut her off, the words spoken deeply, coming from his chest or maybe even his very soul.

She lifted her head, needing to read those dark, fathomless eyes of his to see the truth in his words for herself. He met her gaze, clearly meaning every word of it.

"Really?" she breathed, barely able to believe her luck.

He nodded as he cupped her face and drew her mouth to his for a sweet, perfect kiss. It felt like a blessing or sealing of their fates and lives being interwoven together, forever. Relief coursed through her body, making her legs shake from the sheer thrill of him feeling as deeply committed as she.

Kimber wrapped her arms tightly around Tristan and held him close, burying her head in his chest and nearly shouting with joy. He held her just as firmly, as if he would never let her go.

"I'm exhausted," she said. "Do you want to come back to my place? Get some rest?"

"Darling, if you genuinely want a full four hours of sleep then don't invite me over," Tristan said.

She chuckled, torn and not certain of how to react. She loathed the thought of spending her down time so near yet so far away from Tristan, but she didn't want to push or cling to him. Thankfully, he continued.

"Of course, if you're happy with two hours of sleep and two hours of free rein explorations, then I'd love to come back to your place and show you a thing or two."

Chuckling, she lifted her head to his. Pressing their lips together, she kissed him slowly, enjoying the indulgence of being able to explore his mouth fully with her tongue. After a moment they pulled very slightly away, only inches.

"I think I can manage on a few hours' sleep," she murmured. "I'd much rather spend my free time exploring you than sleeping any day. It sounds like Preston means to keep you busy when you return, and after all the reports and such are cleared up I'll be returning to my normal, boring lab work anyway. It would be terribly wasteful for me to sleep for four hours when we can both manage on two."

"Mmm," Tristan agreed. "What did you have in mind?"

"Well," she teased, drawing the word out slowly. "I've been known to be a wonderful breakfast chef and my flat has this enormous marble-topped kitchen bench..."

"Oh yeah, baby," he muttered huskily. "I'm a sucker for bacon and eggs, or maybe a Spanish omelette."

"I'll even throw in some French toast," she promised. "I can think of some interesting things I'd like covered in maple syrup."

"Sold," he replied, bending his head to kiss her fiercely once again. Nipples tightening Kimber lifted herself up on her tiptoes to wrap her arms around his neck and pull their bodies flush together. Her clit tingled in anticipation and her pussy grew slick with need.

When they were both panting Tristan braced a hand to the base of her back and lifted his head.

"We better get going or someone's going to walk down here and catch us," he insisted. Kimber nipped a biting little kiss to his full lower lip before stepping way.

"Let's go," she agreed.

"Lead the way," Tristan said. "I promise I'll follow you anywhere."

With a satisfied grin Kimber took his hand in hers, threading their fingers together and headed for the door. They might not have had a lot of time right then, but there was the rest of their lives ahead of them. She figured it was plenty of time for many more adventures.

PASSIONATE
VENGEANCE

Dedication

With love and thanks to the Lovely Lily.

Prologue

Abigail Turner wondered how long she had been in this fiery hellhole. Caught up in the ceaseless torment, reality and her dreams had mingled long ago. Time had lost all meaning. Her world—or what she managed to understand of it—had narrowed to the here and now, to every appalling second.

She shifted uncomfortably, the simple motion sending screaming agony across her tortured body.

The room was so bloody hot!

Her body ached in every muscle, nerve and sinew. It felt like she had tried to find a restful position for hours, but no matter what contortions she attempted, nothing assuaged the pain.

Groaning, she moved again, Abby twitched. Flames shot across the back of her shoulders, licking their way over her skin and deeper still. Stiffly she tried to ease the pain by moving her joints in a circular fashion. She hoped to relieve some of the pressure. But the motion sent more jolts down her back and up her neck. The dull throb whipped up to her skull and started to form a painful headache.

The temperature was unbearable, sweltering in its intensity. Ironically, she usually enjoyed the heat, but this far outstripped anything she had ever experienced. This was not the heartening warmth of a hot summer's day, but the endless, ceaselessly sweating heat of being too close to an out-of-control fire.

Sweat pooled at her collar, and her clothes stuck to her skin. Each breath was agonising. Abby felt the flames cover her skin. When a cramp squeezed her with particular intensity she couldn't stop the screams from ripping through her lungs and falling from her raw, parched throat.

'Stop it!' the voices whispered to her. *'They'll hear you and come back.'*

Abigail couldn't remember precisely who 'they' were and where she was that would allow them to come 'back', but nevertheless fear took hold of her. The voice had been insistent this time and she was certain nothing good could come from ignoring the inner warning.

And so she endured the pain, stoically continued to withstand the heat of the fire raging inside and around her. Tears leaked from her eyes, the cramps becoming unbearable. Never before had she wanted to be a heroine—she'd not wished for fame or glory, for martyrdom or to be anything other than her normal self. She'd never wanted to push her limits or achieve the unbelievable.

Weeping, Abigail reached out with her heart and soul, desperate for relief. Taking in one shuddering breath after another, she closed her eyes and mind against the unendurable pain and wished for death to come and claim her.

* * * *

Each breath continued to be painful. Fire consumed her, burning her lungs, decaying her muscles one cell at a time. She could no longer help it.

Abigail screamed. Over and over.

Just as the voices had warned her, 'they' came. Lost in her own world of misery she barely registered it. They hurt her more, but it was pinpricks compared to what already overwhelmed her.

And still the fire raged, consuming her body and soul, desperate to overtake her.

Sheer stubbornness had her holding on now, nothing else.

At one stage she could hear bells tolling in the distance. Her death knell, she wondered? Too tired to care, too wrung dry to do anything except breathe in and out over and over, she waited for the end to come.

It refused.

The pain continued, the flames fanned higher.

The voices whispered continuously to her now. She had learnt hours — days? — ago to block them out. In her weaker moments, when she feared she'd been abandoned by all those around her, she would listen once again to them. Just to assure herself she wasn't ever truly alone.

'…Abigail never applies herself as she should…'

'…such a delightful girl — if only she'd pay attention when we…'

'…and then she said…'

'…she never…what is wrong with her…?'

'…follow your heart, Abby, trust in what you know is true…'

The last voice she recognised. It was her grandmother's. She struggled to follow her — it felt like forever since she'd been held in a hug or snuggled close to the warm familiarity of her gran.

Her body refused to obey her, and no matter how hard Abby looked she couldn't see clearly. Then those bloody bells interrupted once again, deafening her and making her cower down, hands pressed over her ears to drown out the sound.

As always, the pain returned. Her muscles seized up once again and the jolts thundered through her body. Flames that must surely be from the fires of hell licked along the line of her back, her skin feeling as if it were being ripped from her flesh.

Abigail desperately wished for a moment's clarity, just a few seconds to think and make a plan for herself. But the pain encompassed everything and she floundered.

* * * *

She had no idea how much time had passed — minutes, hours or days. Time had ceased to have meaning to her.

A knight came towards her. He wore spaulders, a knight's chest armour that also covered his shoulders and upper arms. The silver shone in places as if it had been recently polished, though paradoxically it also remained tarnished in other sections, showing its age and copious wear.

He stalked through the fires, neither flinching nor protecting himself from the flames as they raced over his body.

"Help me!" Abigail cried out. Her arms refused to move, though she wished she could wave and capture his attention.

Her voice croaked with disuse — or perhaps it was the strain of speaking after her screams and tears. Pain racked every muscle, the heat overwhelming her as sweat pooled around her body. Exhaustion battered her, the effort to breathe and stay conscious taking every ounce of energy she possessed.

Abigail tried to focus on the knight as he continued towards her. Caucasian, blond, tall, everything else was a blur. Her eyes were failing. The harder she struggled to look, the less he fell into focus. Drained of all energy now, Abby feared that this would be it. Surely the knight wasn't there for her? He'd pass her, not even realising she lay there in a heap, collapsed within the endless flames.

She came to understand this would be the end. She would have to embrace death, give up her monumental struggle at last.

She saw the knight reach her in the seconds before her eyes fluttered shut. He bent down. His blond hair shielded his face and softly caressed the skin of her forehead. He collected her up in his strong arms. She moaned when he wrapped her body firmly in his arms, clasping her to his chest—he didn't seem to mind lifting her weight at all. The motion was smooth, as if she were as light as a child.

Abigail collapsed against his warm solidness, her head cradled in the hollow of his neck. She couldn't believe he'd found her, saved her at her most critical moment.

"Are you real?" she murmured, her voice hoarse from crying, screaming, and hour upon hour of tears.

"Not yet," he whispered to her. "But soon I will be."

In her deluded exhaustion Abby didn't even understand the meaning behind his words. She simply understood the comfort of not bearing this impossible load alone anymore. His presence soothed her beyond belief. He battled the flames with her, and inexorably he helped her force them back, even just a little way.

Abigail Turner fell into a fitful but genuine sleep at last.

Chapter One

"Impress me, George." Lucas Sloan pushed one hand down on the wiry tech's shoulder and leaned in close.

George ran a hand through his messy brown hair and pushed it out of his eyes.

Lucas smirked and tried to read the man's laptop screen over his shoulder.

"You really need a haircut," Lucas teased.

"I thought Jones ordered you and Walters to take four hours down time before you showed your faces back here?" George complained, though there had been no real sting to his tone.

Lucas shrugged and pushed aside the oppressive feeling of worry and doom that had haunted him the last day or so.

"Keep your voice down, mate," Lucas snapped as he cast a quick look around to make sure no one had overheard him. "Preston did order Tristan and I to take a few hours' rest before we hit this again. You announcing to the world I'm here will just get me in deep shit. So shut it, all right?"

George chuckled, seeming unconcerned by his ire.

"Everyone is hard at work helping you and your partner solve this case," George said with evident amusement. "While you and Tristan get your beauty sleep, we're all back at the grindstone. No one will tattle on you for coming in an hour early. You got my message, I presume?"

"I couldn't sleep," Lucas explained. He hesitated, searching George's expression before continuing. "I don't know if it's because this is my first real case — not just with Tristan as my partner, but my first real mission — but it's hit me hard, really got under my skin. This girl we're searching for, Abigail Turner, you know she's been injected with some sort of super-vaccine? Something that crazy Dr Harper and an ex-Manager of the Agency, Emma Henley cooked up to do heaven knows what with. They've injected her with it multiple times. All the other test subjects have died over the last six months and now she's missing. How am I supposed to take 'down time' with all this going on?"

"Tristan Walters didn't have much trouble with it," George teased him.

Lucas shook his head impatiently. "Don't be fooled by that calm, suave demeanour of his," he warned. "He only went back to his flat to settle Kimber. She might appear all blonde curls and laughter behind that brilliant brain of hers, but she was exhausted, mentally and physically. Tristan has fallen hard for her and protecting Kimber comes naturally as breathing to him now. He left only so she could rest. Otherwise he'd be hiding out here trying to find this poor girl with me."

"Sounds to me like Tristan isn't the only one falling around here," George chuckled.

Lucas narrowed his eyes, his heart pounding. *Don't be a fool*, he insisted, *George can't possibly know about that dream you had when you nodded off in the car. Get a grip, Sloan!*

"Don't be ridiculous," Lucas snapped, more annoyed at the truth behind George's words than his friend actually speaking the thought aloud. "I haven't even met the girl yet, I can't possibly have feelings for her. I sympathise with the shit she's going through and want to help her. That's it."

George threw him a sympathetic look. Lucas frowned, not sure he was pleased to have been baited into speaking so defensively. George remained thankfully silent, seeming to be happy to leave his teasing at that.

"I've only been here six months longer than you, mate," George changed the subject. "And take it from me, the first few cases are the ones that really grab you by the throat. Just a word of caution, if Jones or any of your superiors feel you're getting in too deep you'll be relegated to the mailroom. If they tell you to take a break, take it. If you're ordered to back off something you better have a really good reason or irrefutable proof to support you if you go against orders. Old hands like Walters can get away with shit because they've earned their reputations and have brass balls. Everyone knows Walters and those like him are solid agents and if they break the rules it's for a bloody good reason. Right now you're not just a newbie but an unknown. Earn your rep and then play fast and loose with the rules."

Lucas nodded, knowing what George had said was nothing less than the truth, but something about this case had a hold on him. The vulnerability he could feel in these victims, Abigail Turner in particular, had crawled under his skin and wouldn't leave him.

Before the meeting where Preston had ordered him, Kimber and Tristan to take a rest, George had shown him Abigail's driver's licence and photo. Pale skin with green eyes and strawberry-blonde hair falling below her shoulders, she'd looked beautiful and haunted.

When Lucas had taken a brief nap in his car he'd dreamt of Abigail, lying crumpled on the ground, her hair covering her face as her slender body shook with sobs. She lay in a ring of fire calling out for help with the desperation only the truly needy could ever use.

He couldn't go home and lie in his bed, pretending this was a regular case. Something urged him that time was of the essence, and he wasn't used to denying his gut feelings. They'd been right far too often.

He sighed and ran a hand through his hair, ignoring the way parts spiked up and others fell into his eyes.

"Okay, mate," he placated George, who was merely trying to assist him. "I read you loud and clear. Once you've told me what you found I'll go to the lockers and lie down on the cot bed there. Promise. Just assuage my curiosity now you've piqued it. What have you found?"

George smirked. Satisfaction gleamed in his dark eyes, the kind that came from achieving a truly remarkable feat. Lucas knew the man well enough to understand George had pulled something wizardly out of his computer.

Anticipation hummed in Lucas' blood. He scanned the data on George's screen once again and tried to make sense out of it.

"Kimber's suggestion that we search to see if the subject tried to get a second opinion on her medical condition hit pay dirt. Your girl Abigail went to another clinic a little over forty-eight hours ago complaining of a mild fever and what she believed to be an allergic reaction to a recent vaccine. Her records had been wiped, which made me curious to say the least. So I did the smallest bit of hacking into the clinic's security system and found this."

With obvious pride, George clicked on a small video clip and maximised it on the screen. Lucas watched, his breath catching in his throat as Abigail was forcibly led out of the back door and to a waiting medical van. Two burly orderlies flanked her and pushed her roughly into the vehicle when she balked and started to struggle.

Lucas leaned closer and tried to read the licence plates, frustrated when the grainy feed from the video made that impossible.

"Damn it all to hell," he cursed and hit his palm on the desk to vent his annoyance. "Replay it, George, I want to — "

"Find the van. Yes, Lucas, you're not the only person in this agency who wants to help that woman," George replied wryly.

He clicked open another tab and the van came onto the screen, its registration details and paperwork all rendered visible.

"I'm not a complete moron," George said.

Lucas looked to his friend and smiled. "I owe you a beer next time we're down at the local, mate. I apologise for ever doubting you," he replied as he scrambled for a pen to write the details of the van down.

"You owe me a six pack, mate," George said smartly, picking up a sheet of neatly folded paper sitting on his desk beneath a notepad. "The van is registered to a private clinic situated just outside Basildon. While Abigail Turner is not officially listed as one of their current residents, I called one of the day nurses and sweet talked her—that's why you owe me the good stuff, mate—and a thirty-year-old strawberry-blonde woman was admitted for a seventy-two hour lockdown watch as a favour to one of the doctor's friends. Dr Paul Harper."

"You're fantastic," Lucas thanked him. "Have you sent this to Preston? I can call Tristan and we can move on it right away."

"If a doctor has ordered a suicide watch on Turner then it would be illegal to remove her from professional custody," George said.

Lucas bit back the instant retort that sprang to his lips, thinking for a moment before replying. It only took a second to understand his friend's true warning.

"You mean we will have to go in dark? Kidnap her to free her, effectively?"

George nodded, his face serious.

"That's why I called you. Preston Jones is new. I've not worked directly with him as yet. After the debacle surrounding Henley turning out to be a traitor I—well, I wanted to be certain informing your superior was the right move."

Warmth and gratitude flooded Lucas. He grinned and clasped George's shoulder in thanks.

"You really are the best, mate, I mean that," Lucas replied with conviction. "Preston is okay. Send him the data and recommendation I'm betting you've already written up. Besides, you have my word, even if Jones sends it up the chain and we're delayed or screwed over, Tristan is my partner. The two of us can go rogue if it comes to that and rescue Abigail ourselves. This is not the time to let paperwork and red tape interfere with doing the right thing."

"I can see your reputation for being a hot-headed cowboy already building itself." George laughed. He maximised an email with attachments already prepared and clicked 'send'.

Lucas laughed.

"You knew full well what I'd say, didn't you, mate?"

"My IQ isn't this high because I have a pretty face," George countered easily.

They shook hands and as Lucas pulled out his mobile phone he stalked away to call Tristan. Hitting the speed dial, Lucas put the device to his ear and heard Tristan's ringtone sound from the other side of the room. Rushing towards where their desks faced each other, he saw his partner in crisply ironed pants, a fresh shirt, his hair damp from a recent shower.

Disconnecting the call, he pocketed the phone just as Tristan answered it, Lucas spoke.

"I thought we still had at least another forty-five minutes of down time. I've been laying low trying to not get my arse reamed for disobeying orders. I felt certain you'd be snug in bed playing footsie with Kimber. What's happened?"

"I managed an hour's sleep before Kimber's phone rang and results of the testing she put into action started coming in," Tristan replied with a self-satisfied grin. "Since she was up and muttering laboratory type stuff to herself, I got a shower, then decided that sitting around the flat was pointless when she evidently was busy. I decided I might as well be around here. What's your excuse?"

"I couldn't sleep, so I thought if I hung around here keeping out of trouble I'd be set for when the action picked up. Is everything okay between you and Kimber? How's she handling the last couple of days?"

"She's perfect," Tristan replied, a sappy smile spreading over his face.

Lucas grinned, knowing there would be ample opportunity to tease his partner in the future.

"She'll be arriving in a few hours. I think she wants to get her reports all lined up and her ducks in a row...you don't really care about all that shit. What did you need to call me about?"

"George has managed to find Abigail for us," Lucas replied urgently. "Kimber was right, a fact which I plan to apologise for snapping at her about earlier. It seems Abby did go for a second medical opinion and somehow Harper found out about it and has now had her committed."

"Abby?" Tristan teased, a glint in his dark eyes.

Lucas made an impatient noise.

His partner continued before Lucas could snap at him. "Where was she committed and what for?"

"A clinic just outside Basildon," Lucas said.

Tristan stood and shrugged into his jacket.

"George has given the details to Jones, but if we're not given the green light soon I wanted to know if you'd get her out with me. Off the books."

"Lucas," Tristan replied with a small chuckle. "The longer you're here, the more you will find practically everything we do here is off the books. Despite that, if we can work with our superiors it cuts the necessary paperwork in half when a case wraps up. But if it comes to it then yes, of course I will kidnap this woman with you, but let's give Preston a chance to read the damn report first, okay?"

Lucas itched to instantly race out but knew what his partner had said made sense.

"Okay, but what about—"

"Walters, Sloan, in my office right now," Preston Jones bellowed from across the room. He had stuck his head outside his office door, leaning out just long enough to shout his wishes before stalking back inside.

Tristan and Lucas exchanged looks then heading over.

"See?" Tristan murmured.

Lucas shrugged as they entered Preston's office.

The large man sat behind his desk, the same suit he'd had on earlier still hanging from his frame. Black hair buzzed short. He scanned his dark eyes quickly along the lines, speed-reading the report in front of him.

"I thought I said four hours," Preston said mildly as he waved for them both to take a seat.

"Sir, with all due respect—" Lucas began but Preston held up a hand to silence him.

"Leave it," he insisted. "I have better things to do with my time than harass you for being passionate about your work. Don't make a habit of ignoring my orders, though. That would be foolish. Do I make myself clear?"

Tristan and Lucas both nodded.

"Right, then let's move on. I assume the two of you were conferring about the new evidence that Abigail Turner is being held against her will in a clinic on a seventy-two-hour suicide watch? Yes, of course you were, I can tell by that guilty look on your face, Sloan. What were you planning? Sloan?"

"Evidently she was placed into custody against her will," Lucas replied, with a quick glance to Tristan to be certain of his support in this.

His partner's gaze remained steady and he tilted his head faintly to indicate Lucas should continue.

"We were hoping that a plan to free her would be put in place that we could activate promptly. Clearly she is an innocent in this and Harper has been taking advantage of her."

"Seems like you're in luck, then," Preston said a wry smile tilting the corner of his mouth up. "I agree with your assessment. I want you to be cautious here, Sloan, you're flirting very close to the edge of being too emotionally invested in this case and this girl. Until we're certain she is an innocent pawn, and not a willing party to Henley and Harper's games I don't want you getting too attached. If I feel your emotions are clouding your judgement, or compromising this case I'll reassign you both faster than you can blink. One step over the line and I'll write you up for insubordination. We clear on that?"

"Yes, sir," they both replied.

Lucas had to swallow down the instinctive and gut-deep reaction of denial. This was *his* case, he needed to rescue this woman.

Even as he thought it, Lucas could see he had already privately stepped over the line of what was proper and what was not. In his heart he knew Tristan had guessed, but nevertheless protected him, and for that he was grateful. Their partnership might have begun as a rocky road, but they had settled into a friendship that only strengthened over time. Lucas wouldn't want to test that newly blossoming relationship with too much weight at this early stage, but for now he decided he could trust Tristan to back him up.

"I understand that your first priority will be to get this girl out of the clinic and safe," Jones said, his deep voice firm and serious. "But I need to give more than that to the higher-ups. If they have her under psych evaluation she might be doped to the gills on meds, in who knows what kind of physical and mental state. Questioning her immediately might need to take a back seat to the Agency medics doing their job and keeping her well."

"You want us to question the staff?" Tristan asked sceptically. "If we're going to be carting off one of their patients—with or without their approval—I doubt that will lend them to standing around placidly answering twenty questions with us."

"No shit," Preston cut back. "I was thinking more along the lines of perhaps one of you getting the girl under control and the other doing something useful, like nosing into their records, seeing what information they have on Dr Harper that might be of use to us. Small, unimportant things like that."

"I can get the guys in tech to set up an external hard drive for us," Lucas suggested. "Since George knows the software they're using over there maybe he can help them get a drive copier installed for us, and instead of leafing through and scouring their drives we can just copy the lot?"

Preston winced but appeared to consider his suggestion for a minute.

"How about you instruct George to set the software up to copy anything related to Harper. What say we try to keep the massive breach of privacy to a minimum?"

Lucas nodded and they were silent a moment.

"Get cracking, men," Preston finished. "It will be dark in just a few hours. I want you back in here with a solid plan before then. Talk to the techs, get whatever equipment you'll need, and be certain you warn the medics they'll have another bed filled, at minimum overnight. Go."

Lucas and Tristan stood and left the office. They crossed to their own desks and sat down in silence. Lucas glanced around the room at the many other agents busily working on their own cases and finally came a full circle back to watch his partner. Tristan's dark gaze remained on him and Lucas sighed.

"What is it?" he asked in a low tone, hoping they weren't going to have a problem. From experience he knew showing mutual support in front of one's superiors was one thing. Privately supporting one another when one party didn't agree with the other was completely different. While Tristan might be perfectly willing to not rat him out to Preston, whether his partner thought he'd lost his marbles in private could still make things uncomfortable between them.

"When we were assigned together after Peterson was murdered I did some checking on you." Tristan's response surprised Lucas. He kept silent, waiting for Tristan to continue with what he needed to say. "Despite the fact it took us a while to find our pace together I knew from the start you were a good man, and after the first few weeks I could tell you'd make a damn fine agent."

Tristan's words caused Lucas to lift his eyebrows and a smile blossomed across his face. They were friends and partners, but rarely did they so explicitly state their faith in one another. It just wasn't something either really did. Lucas had to admit though, warmth and a kind of gratitude spread in his chest at his partner's words.

"Uh, thanks," he replied. Lucas wasn't quite sure what he was meant to say to that. They nodded at each other. Lucas understood that Tristan was conveying they'd stand side by side whatever might come their way.

"I appreciate it. And I don't need to tell you what a good agent you are, mate. I'm glad we're partners," Lucas said a bit gruffly.

Tristan chuckled as he gathered his notebook and stood. They stared silently for a moment before Tristan seemed to come to some internal decision. He tilted his chin slightly at Lucas in acknowledgement.

Lucas' gut tightened nervously. For a few brief seconds he worried about what exactly his partner had decided.

"Don't fuck this up," Tristan warned him. "I know you're way more invested in this girl than you should be, but frankly I'm not in a position to point fingers. I would have crossed every line imaginable to keep Kimberly safe and be with her like I am right now. I have to side with Jones, though. We don't know anything about Abigail. You haven't even met her. Maybe she is an innocent caught up in a nightmare, but maybe she isn't. I'll protect your back as long as I can, Sloan, but just try to take it easy. And like I said — don't screw this up. It's not just your arse in this fire, but mine too."

Lucas nodded, his friend's warning hitting home far more than Preston's ever could. Jones was their boss, and while he was decent as far as managers went, he still had to keep his eye on the bottom line and kiss the arses of those above him. Tristan wasn't spouting the party line or bullshitting him. His partner was merely trying to slap him with a reality check and Lucas appreciated it.

"I won't get in too deep, I promise," he returned. "Besides, you'll be there in the clinic with me. If I go over the top you can beat me about the head with a stick or something to keep me in check."

"Like you'd listen," Tristan snorted. "I'd have shot anyone who'd tried to stop me being with Kimber. I doubt you'll be any different."

Lucas grinned widely, amused.

"Then I guess I'll just have to not mess this up, won't I?"

Tristan winked at him.

"I'm going to go and chat to the techs, since it doesn't take a rocket scientist to realise I'll be the one scanning the data files and you'll be the one playing knight errant to Ms Turner."

"How did you guess that's how I'd want us to divvy up the tasks?" Lucas teased.

Tristan gave him the finger and left.

Lucas took a deep breath and tried to push the mental picture of long strawberry-blonde hair out of his mind. He could still so clearly visualise her struggling with those two goons, her back arching as she'd tried to wrestle free from their grip while they'd shoved her into the truck.

Trying to calm himself, he instead imagined her straddling him, those long red locks flowing down her back which was bowed in pleasure. He would thrust himself deeply inside her, those pale green eyes piercing him. He'd sheath his cock fully within her tightly clenched pussy. Her warmth would encompass him when she swallowed his dick deeply into her. He imagined her taking him far within her, until his balls slapped against her soft skin.

Panting, Lucas realised too late he'd let his fantasy go too far. His shaft pressed beneath the zipper of his slacks, hard and erect.

"Damn it," he cursed and closed his eyes. This woman had been taken advantage of enough. He didn't need to be fantasising about her, wishing he could hold her and feel the softness of her skin when heaven knew what she's already been put through. Since when was he such an idiot?

Lucas forced his mind away from her. He had to write out the course of action he and Tristan would use in their attempt to rescue Abigail. First there would be the paperwork surrounding a request for the equipment they would need, then — the mental picture of Abigail's large, green eyes filled the darkness behind his closed lids.

Her silky hair fell to either side of her face, her skin pale as porcelain. Lucas could see the tiny smattering of freckles over her nose as she bent down. He was seated and she on her knees before him. She would part those rosy red lips, swallow down around his aching shaft.

In his fantasy she sucked him down like a pro, the heat of her mouth and throat surrounding his cock even better than her dripping cunt. She bobbed her head, her strawberry locks swaying against his legs and falling halfway down the slender line of her naked back. Abigail would flick her tongue out to run it along the head of his shaft, collecting his pearls of cum. She'd then swallowed them down, the motion caressing his cock like a heated fist.

"Fuck it," Lucas stood and stalked to the men's room. He needed release right now. The bloody reports could wait a minute or two. Lucas fully understood he needed to get a hold of himself when it came to this woman, but he was too far gone. Right now he needed to come with an urgency he hadn't felt since he was in his teens.

After he'd finished, then he could write the damn reports and go and rescue this alluring, intoxicating, bloody frustrating woman of his fantasies.

Chapter Two

Abigail still struggled to differentiate between reality and her dreams, though she had to admit over the last twenty-four hours things had cleared up significantly. She no longer thought she was hallucinating being trapped in a nightmarish hell. She now knew that was part of her new reality.

Strapped down to the hospital style bed, Abigail regretted the many horror movies she'd so enjoyed in her youth. And the manner with which the nurses and doctors treated her like an imbecile was insulting, though when she'd tried to point it out to them, she'd been ignored like a naughty child. Worse, Dr Harper had evidently told them she was a threat to herself as much as them.

It was ridiculous. Her world had been turned upside down, and those to whom she would have instinctively approached looking for some help—the nurses, orderlies and doctors who professed to be on her side, for starters—refused to believe her when she'd said she was fine and wanted to go home.

At first she had been calm, trying to explain things.

"I'm not the least suicidal, I just want to go home. I've been unwell and wanted some medicine..."

Pitying glances, murmurs of 'Denial is not the sign of a healthy mind, Abigail', and other condescension had met her rational requests. So she had become frustrated—who wouldn't in similar circumstances?—and she had shouted, had screamed to be let out or at least be able to plead her case with the doctor.

"Who do you think sent you to us for assistance?" had been their reply to that.

When Abigail had gasped, had insisted they'd lied, they had parroted Dr Harper's phone number, email address and personal details to her and had insisted it had been he who had committed her 'for her own good'.

The entire situation was nightmarish. Abigail half believed it had been they who had made her so sick that first night. Certainly she was inundated with crazy, frightening dreams every time she fell into an exhausted sleep—or worse, when they sedated her, but if she'd had a fever earlier it had long passed and now she simply wanted to get out of there.

"I'm not crazy, I'm not crazy, I am definitely not crazy," she repeated to herself softly enough to not be overheard. Should one of the nurses, or syringe-happy doctors hear her reassuring herself of such a thing they'd certainly pump her full of their favourite drugs.

Her wrists were chafed raw from her trying to get out of the restraints, but still she tried to tug herself free. Unable to contain the whimper that escaped, she struggled again. Trembling in mingled fear and anger she stopped, realising escape was only a useless fantasy. She tried to compose herself.

Never had she been so helpless before, or so completely at other's mercy. She hadn't wanted to be in a situation like this, but now she knew for a fact she simply couldn't cope with being restrained. She loathed the knowledge that she was so powerless, unable to do so much as scratch her nose should she have the desire. The entire situation sucked and a part of her mind continually screamed in terror.

What would happen should there be a fire? Should someone come in to harm her? She'd not ever before lost her independence so thoroughly. The entire situation petrified her. Abigail breathed slowly, forcing herself to have faith something miraculous would occur.

Calming herself as best as she could, Abby gathered every scrap of information she'd been able to assimilate and overhear. She was being held on a seventy-two-hour suicide watch. Dr Harper was supposed to have come and seen her today, to 'gauge her mental state', but gossip amongst the orderlies who had washed the floor of her room before dinner had indicated something big had occurred at one of his other clinics and he'd been unable to get away.

Part of her was terrified she'd scream and shout at him, lose control totally and he'd have her committed fully. Losing so many of her basic human privileges had her on edge, ready to claw at him, hurt him in the same way he'd managed to hurt her. Yet she knew that way only led to more trouble.

Dr Harper would see her in the morning and she'd state frankly that she would give him whatever it was he wanted, but he had to let her out. Or else.

Abigail couldn't even begin to think of what the doctor wanted from her. She had nothing. No real assets and very little money stashed away into a small savings account. Certainly nothing in any aspect of her life led her to believe anything like this could be possible.

Abby had sworn earlier in the morning that when she got out of there she'd take steps to make her life more worthwhile. She'd always imagined she had plenty of time to date, to get out more with her friends, to watch that movie or attend that party. The fact she'd been so easily coerced into this and completely out of touch for almost forty-eight hours now, and not a single person had come looking for her, was humbling in the extreme.

"Oh, Gran, I miss you so much. You would rescue me, come hell or high water."

Tears filled Abigail's eyes but she blinked them away.

Instinctively she tested the restraints again, refusing to cower and give in, despite her genuine fear. Sooner or later she'd get out of them, and she swore the first thing she'd do would be to cause serious bodily harm to Dr Harper. She imagined punching him in the nose, shooting him through the heart or perhaps sticking him with one of those damned needles, filling him with whatever cocktail of drugs he seemed so entranced with and watching him suffer the nightmares she'd experienced.

She was not some spineless imbecile. This would not get the better of her.

Abigail tugged on her restraints again, ignored the pain in her wrists and plotted vengeance.

* * * *

Breaking into the clinic had been almost embarrassingly easy. Tristan had seen two of the orderlies wedge open a side door with a broken brick. They'd walked around the small car park and had smoked their cigarettes. After hours, the main body of the clinic was closed down and dark, but the few patients were watched over by a skeletal staff of two night nurses, some cleaners and a few other assorted helpers.

Breaking into the clinic had been almost embarrassingly easy, they had slipped in through the open door like it was the most natural thing ever. The two orderlies listened to the footy game on a small radio, arguing and smoking, their backs to the building while they were absorbed in their discussion.

Walking as if they owned the place, they moved down a corridor. Lucas followed Tristan, taking care to be discreet as he checked the rooms they passed. The two nurses sat at the table, both cupping hot drinks. Neither nurse gave them a second glance as they walked by the closet-sized space evidently used as a tea room.

The corridor opened out into the main station area. Lucas lifted the three clipboards and scanned the patient records while Tristan inserted the USB of the portable hard drive into the desktop computer on the nurse's desk.

"She's in bed two," Lucas said softly.

Tristan nodded and checked the monitor of the computer.

"Says here it will take two minutes to download the relevant files," he replied. "You secure Abigail and meet me back here. They might not have paid attention to us coming in, but with her in tow we might have a far harder time getting out."

Lucas watched as Tristan pulled his gun from out of his waistband and placed it on the desk beside him.

"You should get yours out too," Tristan insisted.

Lucas shook his head.

"Not until I have her. If I turn up with a gun I might freak her out."

"Suit yourself." Tristan shrugged. "But don't leave it for long. It will be no use to you hidden away if you need it."

Lucas nodded and put the clipboard back before heading into the adjoining room. He found a small waiting area, presumably for friends and family. Passing through an open door he found three small, locked doors with 'Room 1', 'Room 2' and 'Room 3' stencilled on each of them. Hazarding a guess, he looked through the window into Room 2, unsurprised to see Abigail lying in the bed.

Disgusted to find her forcibly tied down onto the thin hospital mattress, he barged inside without any warning. She jerked her head up, fright widening her eyes.

"Who are you? What are you doing? No! Don't come near me! Please, you can't inject me again. I've been good, please!"

Her voice sounded hoarse. Lucas could tell she wanted to scream and plead, to make a ruckus, but her throat was raw. Her words made little sound despite her obvious intentions otherwise.

"Shhh," he cautioned her, his heart bleeding for this poor woman. He hated the thought of her harming herself further. "You're safe now, I promise. My name is Lucas. I'm here to get you out of here."

Quickly, he unbuckled the straps restraining her left hand. Abigail watched him silently, but he saw the pulse in her neck beating a rapid staccato. He didn't blame her for being scared, but if she continued to yell out it would attract unwanted attention, which they could ill afford. Despite the softness of her tone, if she spoke long enough someone would notice. Anger beat at him again. He noticed the red, raw chafing on her wrists. Temper spiked, he had to work to keep it under control and not scare her further.

Those pitiless arseholes, he mentally swore. Part of Lucas wanted to stop what he was doing, go back out to those nurses and orderlies and beat them all senseless. Holding himself in check was difficult, but Abigail's big eyes helped him collect his wild emotions.

Focus on the big picture here, Lucas, he reminded himself. *Free Abigail, vengeance can come later.*

"Abigail, I need you to listen to me. My partner is out there, downloading what information we can about Dr Harper. We need you to answer a lot of questions later, but I have to know if you're able to get out of here unassisted?"

"Questions?" she repeated, clearly confused. "I've only seen Dr Harper a few times, for my iron shots, what could you possibly... What on earth am I saying, of course! I'll answer anything you want, just get me the hell out of here, please."

He began working on her other restraint. Lucas would assist her out of this hellhole regardless of her guilt or innocence. Abigail grunted impatiently, finally pulling the strap free herself as if she could no longer bear to have the leather encasing her abused wrist.

"Thank you," she said on an exhaled breath. "I can't possibly thank you enough for that."

"My pleasure," he replied. "Can you stand?"

"To get out of this place, I would try to fly if I needed to."

Abigail turned sideways, the back of her white hospital gown gaping slightly as she scooted her legs over the side of the bed and edged her way to ease down onto the cool tile floor.

"I hope it doesn't come to that," he joked.

A dry but very real laugh escaped her. She looked at him, then did a quick double-take, frowning thoughtfully. The hand she had begun to hold out to him for assistance snatched back when she cringed away from him.

His heart pounded with worry. Had she been more deeply affected by the strain of the situation than he had realised?

"Abby, what is it?"

"How do you know my name?" she stammered. "I've seen you before. Have we met? How do I know you? You're a part of this, aren't you? What's really going on?"

The tone of her voice rose, taking on a harsh edge. Fear and perhaps paranoia, or maybe faint panic, were clear from her face and higher pitch. Lucas swallowed his momentary annoyance. He strove for patience and a semblance of calm.

"I've never met you before, I swear," he replied quickly, feeling the pressure of each second they lingered. "I know your name because a person who used to work in my company helped fund Dr Harper's research. We only just a few days ago discovered this and have been trying to help those affected. Your name was one of nine on a list. Abigail, I swear to you I'm not a part of the problem here, I am trying to help you."

She lifted her legs up and hugged them to her. She studied him with large green eyes for a few more precious seconds—seconds he feared they could not waste. Just as he debated picking her up and carrying her, she swivelled her legs to the edge of the bed and held her hand out for assistance.

Lucas wondered if she did indeed have some form of mental problem.

"The dream," she murmured.

Lucas took her hand and helped her off the high bed. She stood, clasping the back of her gown closed with her free fingers.

"Excuse me?" he replied, only half paying attention. He led her across the room, then indicated she should pause a moment. As he ducked his head out and checked to see if the passage was still free, she spoke again, more clearly this time.

"I had a dream last night, a nightmare really, due to the fever I was running. You were in it, that's why I felt I recognised you."

Not certain where to even begin with something like that, Lucas remained silent, took her hand again and led her back out.

"I'm really not crazy," she insisted.

Lucas turned to cast a quick look over his shoulder at her. Her eyes were clear, her beautiful hair falling down her back. Even though she was in evident pain, scared and a total wreck, this woman was stunning to him. Lucas felt a fierce protectiveness towards her, but also a strong kick of lust. She was far more beautiful in real life than her licence picture could ever do justice to.

"I believe you," he replied. "Though maybe let's wait to discuss that dream until it's just the two of us, okay?"

"Okay," she agreed.

"You realise we're not supposed to be breaking you out of here, right?" he asked as he pulled his gun out.

Abigail's eyes widened, fear flickering in them for a moment. She seemed to pull herself together quickly.

"They're very speedy with a syringe," she whispered, clearly worried but seeming happy to go along with him, for now at least. "But I haven't seen any indication that they have weapons or will use that kind of force."

"I'm not willing to take chances," Lucas replied.

She swallowed but nodded.

"My partner, Tristan, is out here. He's with us, okay?"

She nodded again and he kept their hands linked as he led her.

"You done, mate?" Lucas called softly.

"Ready when you are," Tristan replied. He came to the other side of Abigail.

Tristan smiled down at the woman. For a moment, jealousy surged within Lucas. He controlled the pang, forcing himself to remember this was his partner and friend, and he acted more out of kindness than interest. Pushing it aside, surprised by the strength of the horrid emotion, he focused on the job at hand.

"I'll take point," Tristan said.

Lucas tilted his head, agreeing. He understood what Tristan was doing. Besides, Lucas was loath to release Abigail's hand and if it came to a shootout he might need to drag or carry her. It made sense for Tristan to go a pace ahead of them both.

Tristan led them back the exact same way they had come. By Lucas' watch it had been less than five minutes since they'd entered. The nurses in the tea room were rinsing their cups and gaped as they saw them.

"Hey!" the older of the two called out when she saw they had Abigail.

Immediately both Tristan and Lucas lifted their guns and pointed them at the two middle-aged women.

"Don't," Lucas said simply. "We're more than prepared to return the favour and restrain you both as you contained this young lady. Either sit down and shut up or we will happily oblige you both."

The one who had said nothing sat down in her chair immediately, looking cowed and shaking slightly. The one who had called out seemed to debate for only a few seconds before joining her friend.

"Go," Tristan said to them softly, holding his body still but moving his eyes around alertly.

Lucas kept his gun raised and tugged Abigail towards the exit, making sure to keep his body between the two nurses and his charge. Abigail was breathing hard as they passed through the room and headed to the door.

"You okay?" Lucas asked again as Tristan followed a pace behind, making certain they were not followed or ambushed.

"This is a lot scarier than I thought it would be back in the room," she confessed. She pushed a few strands of hair out of her face and stood taller. "I'm fine." She seemed to reassure herself as much as them. "I'm fine. We can do this."

"Damn right we can," Tristan confirmed. "You've got plenty of pluck, Abigail. And it will all be easy from here on in."

Lucas pressed a finger to his lips to indicate silence as they reached the still-wedged-open door. Once again Tristan squeezed past them both. His gun was drawn, though aimed at the ground. Looking up and down, he checked out their route. He paused in the doorway, making a clear target of himself but protecting them both in case something went wrong. He stayed there only a second to judge their surroundings then jerked his head to indicate they should follow him.

Reluctantly letting go of Abigail's fingers, Lucas nudged her to follow Tristan and he brought up the rear. Unable to help himself, Lucas kept one palm splayed flat on the base of her spine while he kept his gun steady in his other hand. Tristan walked quickly across the car park, keeping to the edge of the building and the shadows as much as possible. Abigail had to jog to keep pace. She didn't complain at the quick stride, though her breaths became more rapid.

All too soon it became evident why they were hurrying. An alarm sounded from deep within the clinic, a red light on the outside wall started flashing.

"Run!" Tristan shouted at them and immediately they all sprinted.

The two orderlies shouted from behind them and the sound of heavy footsteps slapped over the asphalt. No gunshots rang out, so Lucas jammed his gun into his waistband near the base of his spine and once again took Abigail's hand in his.

"You drive," Lucas panted at Tristan, "we'll take the backseat. I'll cover our arses."

Tristan nodded wordlessly as they rounded a corner. He put on a burst of speed, racing ahead of them both to get to the car.

"The blue one," Lucas indicated to Abigail, who hobbled slightly in her bare feet, clenching her gown closed as they ran.

Tristan had beeped the doors open and already slid into the driver's seat. Lucas glanced over his shoulder. He grimaced. The orderlies were catching up to them.

Not caring about anything except the need to get away, Lucas scooped Abigail up into his arms and almost flew the last two car lengths. Tristan had already leaned over and had opened the back door for them. Lucas heard the engine start up smoothly, the car rumbling with barely restrained power. Lucas bundled Abby into the car and dove in after her.

The moment Lucas made it inside the car, Tristan burned rubber, pulling away from the kerb. Lucas twisted to pull the door shut as they raced down the street, turning corner after corner seemingly at random. Lucas laughed, hardly able to believe they had really done it, and without needing to fire a single shot.

He replaced his gun back into the waistband of his trousers and sat up on the seat. He reached down and tenderly brushed Abigail's hair back. Just as he had imagined, the strands were baby soft and silky smooth. She looked up to him, her green eyes large and vivid against her pale, porcelain-like skin.

"You're safe now," he murmured.

She took a deep breath then nodded.

He cupped his hands around her shoulders and assisted her up so she could sit on the seat.

"I want to go home, please," she said in a small voice.

Lucas looked to Tristan, catching his gaze in the rear-view mirror.

Tristan shook his head once, apologising silently with his eyes.

Lucas sighed and glanced back to Abigail.

She frowned at him, seeming to have caught the exchange between the two men.

"I don't believe this, I trusted you!"

"Abby, please," he pleaded. "We have a lot of questions, and you need to be checked out by a doctor—we have medics on staff. We can't just let you go, surely you understand that? Even if the police had found you wrongfully imprisoned you'd have had to go to the station, make a statement, answer questions and they'd need to write reports. This is no different really."

She eyed him distrustfully, but his reasoning seemed to give her pause. She turned her head to stare out of the window, her jaw and shoulders set in a stubborn line.

"How long will you gentlemen need me to answer your questions?" she asked without turning around.

Lucas didn't know whether she was plotting and didn't want him to read it in her eyes, or whether she truly couldn't face him. Either option sat uneasily in his stomach. They both had their own pitfalls.

He shrugged in a slightly defensive gesture, though it was lost on her.

"I couldn't answer that with honesty," he explained. "Almost certainly hours, but it could be much longer if things aren't safe."

"What do you mean?" She continued to keep her face averted, staring at the passing streets.

"Abby, you've been injected with a vaccine we have no knowledge about. We believe all of the other subjects have died from it and—"

"You said that before, back in the clinic," she interjected, whirling around to face him with a frown on her face. "What vaccine? What other 'subjects'? What the hell is going on?"

Lucas sighed and held up a hand to stem her rising questions. Briefly, he explained.

"An audit of a traitor within our agency discovered her putting money into work with Dr Harper which they'd labelled 'Project Immunity'. We found a list of nine names, one of them being yours. Further investigation gave us a sample of your blood, recently taken at Dr Harper's clinic. We tested it and found it full of many diseases and pathogens. Dr Harper had been injecting you regularly with a vaccine, presumably to withstand these diseases and heighten your immune system. We found three other case files of his other patients, all of whom have died in recent months. Dr Harper has gone to ground, our traitor isn't talking and a few hours ago we discovered Harper had forcibly committed you and we instigated your rescue. That's where we're at and you can understand the kinds of questions that are floating around."

Abigail shook her head, clearly speechless.

Lucas gave her a moment to gather herself, noticing Tristan periodically glancing at them both in the mirror. A minute ticked by before she finally spoke again.

"I'm mildly anaemic," she stated dully. "When my regular doctor changed clinics I saw Dr Harper by chance, he was merely the pool doctor who took my consultation when my appointment came up. He ordered a blood test—which is quite common to check the level of my haemoglobin—and a few days later when the results came in he gave me a shot, insisting I come back in three months' time for another one. The following time he gave me a shot first and then took a blood test a few days later to check my levels were still acceptable and it's been like that the few times I've been there since."

"It won't hurt you to get checked over," Lucas urged her.

She twisted her hands together on her lap.

Needing to comfort her, he placed his hand lightly on top of hers. When she didn't pull away a warmth surged through him. Possessiveness consumed him. He loved touching her, even chastely like this.

"Come back with us, let the medics check you over and make certain you're out of danger. Tristan and I can hopefully ask all the questions that will be needed and we can write up the reports as quickly as possible. Won't you feel better knowing there's nothing wrong?" Lucas cajoled.

She met his gaze and a tiny smile tilted one corner of her mouth.

"Maybe," she conceded. "But I'd feel even better in my own clothes and not this scrap."

"You look stunning," Lucas promised her. He kept his gaze on hers, the heat in his eyes clearly proving he meant what he'd said.

"Can we at least swing by my place for a change of clothes? You can both come with me if you think I might make a run for it."

Lucas turned to trade glances with Tristan. His partner appeared thoughtful for a moment, then shrugged and spoke for the first time.

"Five minutes won't make a bit of difference in the scheme of things," he acknowledged.

Lucas laced his fingers through Abigail's and squeezed gently. She smiled back at him, gratitude shining in her green eyes.

"Thanks," she said softly, her gaze holding his.

Lucas' heart hammered. Despite the gravity of the situation he couldn't help but be pleased to have calmed her down and answered some of her questions.

"You'll need to give Tristan directions." He tilted his head as he grinned at Abby. "Your address was in Harper's files, but my partner has a terrible sense of direction."

"Bullshit," Tristan replied without missing a beat. "You're the one who had to do a map-search online to find the damn clinic. And then write out the directions onto a piece of paper."

"So you saying you don't want Abigail to give us directions to her place?" Lucas winked at Abigail, knowing full well his partner would need them.

Tristan muttered darkly for a moment before sighing. The banter had brought a chuckle out of Abby and her grin was blinding in its intensity and beauty.

"Fine, give me the bloody directions," Tristan capitulated.

Abigail shifted to settle herself more comfortably on the seat and looked around them to get her bearings.

"Okay…"

Chapter Three

Abby could barely believe after everything that had occurred she once again sat on a gurney-style bed, surrounded by hospital smells and medical equipment having her blood drawn. Maybe she really was crazy after all.

At least she felt infinitely more comfortable in her favourite pair of worn jeans and a bright green T-shirt with the slogan 'Smile big, Run fast, Live Life!' on it. She had hoped the peppy shirt would cheer her mood up, and to a degree it had helped.

The man lounging against one stark white wall also contributed far more to her peace of mind than she cared to admit. Lucas Sloan. She rolled the name around in her head a few more times, liking the way it sounded far too much.

Focusing on Lucas, she found, distracted her from the anxiety that simmered under the surface of her brain. She'd known her life had taken a drastic turn when she'd been bundled unceremoniously into the back of a truck and whisked away against her will. The night of fever and dreams that had followed had disoriented her, then waking up to find herself strapped down in a strange bed, nurses sedating her every time she'd asked too many questions, had all been utterly overwhelming.

Finally having the time, space and mental clarity to think had only given her more questions that needed answering.

"Press down," she was told by the man as he withdrew the needle and collected his various test tubes.

Abigail put her fingers over the tuft of cotton in the juncture of her elbow and pushed to stop the small prick in her skin from bleeding.

The technician met her eyes and smiled in a reassuring manner, then whisked the samples away, presumably for testing. A part of Abigail wondered what they'd find, but she knew very firmly she would not be returning to a hospital unless it became dire. She was done with hospitals and the medical profession.

If they looked hard enough they could find many problems with the healthiest of people. Abigail resolved there and then to trust her own instincts. Unless she were truly unwell she could take care of herself from here on in.

"I guess you're sick of talking by now?" Lucas broke the silence.

She looked towards him, a smile blossoming on her face.

"I'm grateful you and Tristan insisted to your boss that it be the two of you who questioned me and got my story," she replied. "I'm not sure I would have enjoyed going over the same facts three times with complete strangers. And then coming down here and having more tests, more needles…it's not shaping up to be the best night I've ever experienced, no."

"You've been fantastic." Lucas moved towards her and sat gingerly on the edge of the mattress. The way he treated her so gently, as if she would break, proved to her he didn't seem certain how robust her mental and emotional health was. She wanted to feel irritated but knew that response would be the height of hypocrisy. She'd been through a lot and it wasn't unfathomable for him to think she might go off at the deep end. She refused to let his caution upset her, determined to show him through her words and actions that while not at her best, she could handle this.

Abigail shifted so they could look at each other without twisting their necks.

"So what happens now?" she asked. "Is it as simple as I'm allowed to go home? Can you tell me what you guys plan to do next?"

"I don't think it's a big secret," Lucas replied thoughtfully.

He ran a hand through his blond hair and Abigail found it cute how the strands continued to fall partially into his eyes. He flicked them back with an impatient gesture, only to have them slide back again.

"The Agency is willing to put a lot of effort into finding Dr Harper and bringing him to justice," Lucas continued. "Part of this is because our medical techs are salivating at the thought of going over his research and data, possibly gleaning any new evidence into immune resistance he might have uncovered. More importantly, none of us want someone as immoral as Harper running around using unsuspecting humans as guinea pigs for his personal projects."

"So your company wants to continue Dr Harper's work?" Abigail repeated with a sinking sensation in her stomach.

Lucas reached out to touch her shoulder and shook his head vehemently.

"No, no, don't misunderstand me. They won't be replicating his work at all. Kimber assured Tristan that scientists often read up on journal articles that get published in their particular field. Work that one person does might offer an idea or nugget of information to assist a different project. Harper's methods and actions are reprehensible, but some of the structure of his ideas or hypothesis might help give a new direction to currently stalled research. I don't really understand the tech stuff, but what if something Harper has postulated gives a good scientist an idea on their own project, and a vaccine to help cure cancer, or AIDS comes from it? Should we ignore that idea just because Harper is evil?"

Abigail sighed and looked away for a moment as she thought. She had so much in her brain right then it was difficult to think straight.

"Evil is a strong word," she finally said. "Misguided, maybe. Driven, absolutely. I don't condone what Dr Harper has done to me in the least, and I would be outraged if he were allowed to continue, but maybe in his own twisted way he's trying to do this for the right reasons."

"You're defending him?" Lucas replied, clearly stunned.

Abigail shook her head and glanced back at him.

"Absolutely not, but I've met the man. He didn't strike me as a mad doctor, out to kill people without any regard. He certainly seemed single minded, not to mention distracted by his own thoughts, but I'm not sure I would classify him as evil."

They both fell silent for a moment.

"What happens to the blood samples I just gave? What tests are they going to perform?" Abigail couldn't help the vague paranoia and worry that filled her. Having been burnt, she now found it hard to trust in the general goodwill of humankind. She hoped after a bit of time that innate faith would be restored to her once again, that it hadn't been ripped from her forever.

"I can find out," Lucas promised. He took her hand in his and a flutter of warmth shoot through her stomach. She wanted to trust him, to put her faith completely in his hands. Abigail found she wasn't quite there yet, but oh how she was tempted! Lucas' electric blue eyes bored into hers. The desperate desire to believe everything of him, to leave her cares and troubles behind overcame her.

"I just don't want to be poked and prodded again," she insisted in a soft tone. "I don't care if they find my blood full of diseases again. I feel fine. I don't have that fever anymore. I don't feel sick or uncomfortable. I don't care what traditional medical science says, if I'm not showing the symptoms of being sick or feeling wretched then I don't want to be near a doctor or hospital."

"That's completely understandable." Lucas' warm, charming smile made her heart hammer and her stomach knot. The man was irresistible. How did he not have dozens of women draping themselves over him or casting their hearts at his feet? Surely she wasn't the only woman around here with eyes in her head?

"Why don't I go and talk to Dr Morrison and see if they're happy to release you? I bet you're desperate for a shower and to get some rest in the comfort of your own bed."

Abigail clung to Lucas' hand as he made to stand.

He paused, turning to her with a quizzical look.

Her actions surprised her. Not thirty seconds ago she would have loved to have been released, allowed go her own way and try to settle back into her regular life. When it came to that point, however, a new understanding settled on her. She didn't want to sit back and let everyone around her do the work. Abby no longer wanted to rely on other people to make this right. How could she possibly sit at home, or return to her dreary insurance job, or try to lie quietly and sleep when there was still so much left unanswered?

"I want to go with you," she spoke firmly.

Lucas appeared startled, and she couldn't blame him. Up until now the man had only seen her at her very weakest and worst. How could he possibly know she usually was not some weeping, spineless little miss?

Abigail swallowed and repeated herself in a strong tone, determined to start down the road of reclaiming her spirit right there and then. "I'm coming with you," she said more forcefully, determined in her chosen course of action now she'd made it.

"Um, well okay," he replied. "Morrison should just be in his office. It's right down the corridor. We can—"

"No, I don't mean that," she replied with a small laugh. Despite herself she indulged for a moment in his understandable misinterpretation of her words. She giggled, enjoying the way the humour bubbled through her. It felt like forever since she'd laughed like this. Lucas' answering grin seemed instinctive— the natural inclination of one person to find solace with another in a joke—not as if he actually understood why she found this funny.

"I mean I don't want to go home, hide behind the closed blinds and wait for this to be resolved. I'm sure you will be watching Dr Harper and will see this resolved, but I don't want to be hanging around, waiting for you to call and tell me everything is well. I want to help you. And Tristan," she added, almost as an afterthought, "I know you must think me the weakest, most paltry creature alive, but I don't want to sit on my hands doing nothing. I want to help you both. And I can. If you're truly going to search for Harper I'm sure I won't be a burden."

"I... You... Well hell, I'm impressed, Abby. And no one here thinks you're weak or a burden. You've been through a lot and seem to be bouncing back really well," Lucas stuttered.

The admiring glance he gave her eased the stirring of nerves that had already started in her belly. She grinned shyly.

"I'm not a superhero," she warned him. "But I really want to do this. Help out. Be involved."

"I think that would be wonderful," Lucas assured her. "I'm sure Jones and Tristan will be really happy to have the extra help and insight you can give us. I can't imagine either of them will have a problem with you hanging around. As you said, you're the only one who's met Harper, who knows him."

Warmth spread through Abigail at his words. It had been a spur-of-the-moment decision, but she could feel its rightness deep within her.

'...follow your heart, Abby, trust in what you know is true...'

Abigail re-heard the memory of her gran's words, and she nodded as if the elderly widow stood right before her.

I will, Gran, she promised. *You're right, as usual.*

Abigail ran a hand through the soft strands of Lucas' blond hair, brushing it back from his eyes as she mentally weighed the attraction that simmered between them. Before she could second-guess herself, she leant forward, closing the distance between them on the narrow bed and pressed her lips to his.

Lightning arched when the softness of his lips gave way beneath her own. For a second he seemed frozen, but then he reached up to cup her face in his palms and hungrily kissed her back. Passion rolled lazily in her stomach, a liquid heat she could not possibly deny.

Seemingly of its own volition, her hand raised to press against his chest, the heat from his body singeing her through the thin fabric of his shirt. She moaned, the sound wanton to her own ears. Pressing her body into the heat and warmth him, she enjoyed the weight from his chest pushing back into hers. She craved more contact.

Abigail lowered her hands to his hips, pulling herself up and pushing herself harder into him. Lucas lifted her so she sat partially in his lap. She felt the heated strength of his erection rub along her thigh. Wriggling, she moved against him before lowering her fingers to stroke him through the material of his trousers.

Power surged through her, the feeling not just of finally taking control, but of doing exactly what felt right. Abigail cared deeply for Lucas, not just because he was a hero in her eyes, but because her body reacted so fiercely to him. She craved his touch, his taste and the solid feel of his warmth beneath her fingers.

"Fuck," he groaned as his hips rose up to meet her touch. "You have no idea how much I fantasised about this earlier."

She opened her eyes to stare into his hot blue gaze. Taking his lower lip between her teeth and tugging him gently, she sucked on him. She flicked her tongue over his wet warmth.

"Mmm?" she mumbled before slowly licking and kissing her way along the edge of his jaw.

"Your picture drew me," he muttered huskily, the intensity of his look searing into her. "Those eyes of yours should be declared a lethal weapon. Damn but I want you so badly."

"You have the cutest way of flicking the hair from your eyes. I've wanted you since I first saw you. You were my hero then and still are."

Details from her fever-induced dream came back to her. Despite her ardent desire she didn't think they could literally fuck right there on the gurney where anyone could walk in on them. She instead decided to give him a small piece of her soul as evidence of her trust.

Moving to his side, she sat pressed against the length of his thigh and brushed her finger along his fringe, flicking it out of his eyes. He grinned cheekily at her, his smile warm and making her heart patter.

"When I was really sick with my fever I had a dream about you," she confessed. "I was burning from some sort of fever, about to give up and just let it all take me far away when I saw you coming towards me. You had on this armour, shiny and silver in places and tarnished in others. You picked me up, carried me away from the worst of the pain and flames. I asked if you were real and you said not yet, but you would be soon. You saved me that night as much as you saved me when you released me from that hellhole."

"I want to be your hero, but your villain as well," he whispered with a wicked grin and a delightful twinkle in his eye which thrilled her.

Abigail chuckled and kissed him hard, a long, deeply searching meeting of teeth and tongues. She silently promised with her body what she couldn't yet express in words.

With great reluctance she slowly pulled back, both of them peppering quick, stolen kisses as they moved away. Happiness bubbled inside her heart and chest. Feeling more carefree than she'd ever thought possible again, Abigail winked at him.

"Maybe I should accept that offer to go back home," she suggested, her grin a knowing one.

He brushed his palm lightly across her hair before standing and pulling his shirt tails out from his trousers to hide his slowly receding erection.

"Don't put on the table what you're not willing to go through with," he warned her.

Abigail grinned and slowly stood. "Oh, I'll follow through on all my promises," she assured him. Leaning closer she whispered, "I want to know what you fantasised me doing to you. I might be able to make it a reality."

She watched as Lucas visibly wavered between fulfilling his duty and hopefully just tossing her over his shoulder and carting her somewhere private. Duty appeared to win.

This time, at least.

"Come on." Lucas took her hand and tugged her towards the door. "Let's go and speak to Morrison before I lose what little control I have left."

"What would that entail?" she asked eagerly, a laugh in her tone. "Are we sharing similar thoughts here? You'd spank me? Carry me off over your shoulder? Do tell."

"Never you mind," he ground out, clearly at the limits of his sanity. The hot look he threw her nearly scorched her senses. "I promise to expound later, in intricate detail. Let's tell Morrison you're finished here. You might not believe it but the old bloke seems to have a soft spot for you."

"What?" She gurgled with laughter as they left the room. She dropped her teasing and let him change the subject. "He has the gruffest bedside manner I've ever come across. You can't really expect me to believe he liked me?"

"He offered you one of his mints," Lucas reminded her as she followed him out of the small room and down the hall. "That level of friendliness is practically unheard of for him."

Abigail laughed as Lucas paused outside a door and knocked. Trying to collect herself, she was still chortling when the door opened and Morrison greeted them. His white hair stood up in different directions, giving him the look of the classic distracted scientist. Stubble was smattered along his jaw showed it had been a very long day for him as well.

Despite the lateness of the hour his eyes were clear. Abigail decided Morrison was one of those rare people who thrived on very little sleep.

"Ah, laughter. It's good to hear you're feeling better, Miss Turner. Yes, Sloan, what can I do for you both? Surely not even you expect me to have answers as yet?"

"Uh, no, sir," Lucas replied, clearly taken aback by Morrison's almost jovial tone.

When he seemed to flounder for a moment, Abigail decided to speak up. If she were going to try to assist, she might as well begin immediately.

"I'm planning to help Lucas and Tristan with looking for Dr Harper and wanted to go upstairs and start work on that now. Lucas thought I should just clear that with you first."

Abigail felt alive in a way she'd not experienced in a while. It could be the fact she'd been extremely sick not more than a few days ago and finally thought she could be whole again, or perhaps it was merely the thrill of being so close to a man as potent as Lucas.

Either way, she liked how Lucas made her feel and hoped it could continue well into the future.

"Well physically, my dear, you appear perfectly sound," Morrison spoke as he stepped back and invited them into his small office. "All your vital statistics are fine. We won't know more until your blood tests come back, of course, but I certainly don't see any reason to keep you contained. Do you feel all right?"

"Oh yes." She nodded.

Morrison held his hands up in a universal I-don't-know gesture.

"Until we know more, either from your results or from Harper's notes or the man himself, we really are working in the dark," Morrison explained. "I'd not want you to spend too much time alone, in case you suffer from a reaction we can't foresee. I'd also certainly caution you to take it easy, no running a marathon, for instance. But otherwise I don't see why you can't continue to live your life, young lady."

"She won't be alone," Lucas promised.

Abigail shot him a glance, caught somewhere between blissful happiness and surprise at the possessive tone in his voice. Morrison looked mildly amused.

"Very well, Sloan. You both know where to find me if something comes up."

"Thank you," Abigail said.

Cleared for duty, she followed Lucas out of Morrison's office with a decided spring in her step. She felt amazing, and it was all because of the sexy man in front of her. Her lips still tingled after their kiss. The places on her body his hands had touched remained warm, the passion they'd shared still vivid in her mind and heart.

Her insides still wobbled with fear when she thought about confronting Dr Harper and what he'd potentially done to her—how close she had come to death at his hands. Asserting herself, taking back her own life and making decisions for herself based on her own opinions, had gone a long way towards redeeming her sense of self-control.

The fact this reclaiming had started with a kiss of such intensity it had curled her toes seemed like fate, providence and the best omen possible. Never had she been so instantly smitten with a man, nor had the chemistry been so potent before. Abby could no more have controlled her reactions than she could have changed the course of the sun or moon.

Following Lucas up the stairs to his office, where his colleagues worked, she smiled to herself, knowing in her heart he was easily the best thing that had come from this entire mess. Had she known she'd be given the gift of him at the end of her troubles she'd have willingly chosen to go through the pain and fear she'd experienced in the past few days.

The fact Lucas Sloan had a tight, sleek, firm arse was just a bonus, she decided as she walked behind him. Walking behind him, she ascended the stairs behind that delicious swagger. Even through the material of his trousers she could see the clenching and release of his buttocks.

Oh yes, her hero certainly had an arse to admire.

"I can feel your eyes on me, you know," he said without turning around.

"Are you saying you'd not be doing the exact same thing if our positions were reversed?" she teased him in return.

He laughed and wriggled his arse at her.

Tempted to take a teasing bite, Abigail realised that action lay somewhere out of reach of her newly discovered boldness.

Still, the thought kept her warm while they returned to his desk.

Chapter Four

Abigail pressed a hand to her eyes and tried to still the pounding in her head. Considering how little sleep she'd had in the last few days she could hardly understand how she managed to still be awake at this early hour of the morning. Papers, journal articles, graphs, phone transcripts, bills and an avalanche of paperwork lay spread out on the tables before them all.

She, Kimber, Tristan and Lucas were searching for the proverbial needle in a haystack. Or that's certainly how it felt to Abigail at this moment. Deep in her gut she knew something worthwhile would surface. Dr Harper did not live in a vacuum.

Somewhere in this mammoth sea surrounding his life would be a clue — large or small — to where he had gone, or a hook into how they could run him to ground. It was just up to the four of them and their joint tenacity to unearth and recognise it.

"He has to have a private laboratory somewhere," Kimber muttered.

Part of Abigail wanted to groan. They'd already discussed this, but she had to accept Kimber had a point. The more they went over things hopefully the greater the likelihood some new nugget or train of thought would shake loose.

"Maybe it's not in his name and that's why we can't find it," Abigail suggested. "Does he have an old and trusted friend? Or maybe he rents space. Do you have a contact in the industry who could do a rental search?"

"Aside from Emma Henley I've found nothing indicating he has a partner," Tristan said. "But I like that rental idea, Abby. Kimber, what do you think?"

"Renting space in a laboratory isn't like renting a moving van or piece of gym equipment," Kimber said slowly, clearly thinking the idea through. "But I definitely see where you're coming from. If he still had a mate or old colleague who worked in a lab it would be an easy enough think to borrow a security pass or even just pop on by and ask a favour."

"There can't be that many laboratories in London, can there?" Abigail asked.

"You'd be surprised," Kimber replied. "But let me make a few phone calls. The industry is certainly not large enough that no one can have heard anything if he's sponging from a mate. Someone should mention it sooner or later."

Kimber leaned over to press a chaste kiss to Tristan's cheek before standing with evident relief to be escaping the papers. Abigail watched her go to a nearby desk, seat herself beside a phone and start to punch in a set of numbers. Reluctantly she returned her attention to the two desks they had pushed together and the pile of data still awaiting them.

With a last look back to Kimber, Abigail sighed and picked up the next series of stapled sheets. A glance showed her it was Harper's credit card statement for the month of October the previous year.

"Holy shit," she grumbled, "I should have offered to help Kimber make those calls."

"I think this certainly means we need some more tea," Tristan agreed as he stood up. "Lucas?"

"Yeah, please. White with one sugar."

"Abigail? Would you like a mug?" Tristan asked turning his head to include her. "I plan to boil a new kettle, so there will be plenty."

"Please," she replied with relief at the thought of anything to keep her awake and something to help keep her mind focused. "I take mine black. Thank you."

Tristan stretched, then walked out of the conference room heading for the small kitchenette.

Abby placed the statement back onto the table, rubbed her eyes again and sighed while Lucas leaned over and gently rubbed her shoulders. The firm kneading motion eased knots of tension she hadn't even realised were clustered around her neck and back.

"That feels blissful." She sighed.

They were comfortably silent together for a moment while he massaged her aching muscles. Abigail closed her eyes and the relaxing, calming sensation of Lucas' hands on her had her almost nodding off. She jerked reflexively upright when her head began to dip, jolting herself awake in her seat.

"You should go lie down," Lucas whispered as he pressed a kiss to her temple.

She shook her head stubbornly. "No. I promised I'd not be a burden and I won't go and rest while everyone else is here burning the midnight oil."

"There's a fine line between tenacious and hard-headed," he warned her.

Abigail tilted her head up and back so she could grin at him. "I'm sure you'll either carry me off to bed or I'll fall asleep right here at the desk before I cross the line from one into the other."

Lucas bent down and kissed her tenderly on the lips. Abigail's heart fluttered and heat pooled between her thighs. Her knickers became hot, tight and damp.

"Mmm," he muttered. "I might just throw you over my shoulder and carry you to bed anyway. There are a few discreet places with cot beds already set up. It's not at all unusual for us to pull all-nighters and get a bit of sleep whenever it's possible. I'm sure I could find a suitably private spot for us to…rest."

Lucas knelt in front of her chair. Abigail opened her legs and he settled himself between them. He lifted his arms to wrap them around her and she raised her hands to pull him closer.

Their lips met in a litany of small kisses. Over and over they tasted each other as if for the very first time and they could not get enough. She knew she could never get tired of the way he kissed her, as if he not only enjoyed it but craved it too.

She felt safe in his arms, secure. Nothing in the outside world could possibly matter when he held her and their lips touched. Time slowed and soon had no meaning at all. Abigail could have stayed right in this moment forever and not held a single complaint. Lucas lifted a hand to stroke a few locks of her hair out of her eyes, mimicking the gesture that had elicited such a warm reception last time.

"Tristan will be back soon," he murmured.

Abigail sighed, her eyes slowly fluttering open as if she were waking from a delicious dream.

"I guess we shouldn't embarrass him too much, should we?"

Lucas chuckled.

"Personally I think we could show him a thing or two, but he's my partner and I'd hate to offend his delicate sensibilities."

Abigail laughed at this, but knowing they really did have to get back to it soon, she wrapped her arms around Lucas' shoulders and drew him in for a warm hug. They were still pressed together when Tristan walked into the room bearing a steaming pot of fresh tea and a handful of mugs for them.

Tristan caught her eye first and winked. As he passed, Tristan stuck out his foot and nudged Lucas' ass.

"Enough slacking, mate. Let's get back to it or we'll still be going cross-eyed over these papers when the sun rises."

Lucas wordlessly flipped his middle finger at Tristan. Taking his time, Lucas slowly stood then poured them all a mug of tea, leaving Tristan's in front of him and handing Abigail hers. Lucas pressed a light kiss on her forehead.

"Drink up, darling," Lucas said. "Looks like it's going to be a long night."

Each of them sighing to varying degrees at the truth in those words. Drinking their tea, they continued to search.

* * * *

Dr Paul Harper stood just in front of her, clearly visible yet just inches out of her reach. They were surrounded by a laboratory, filled with clinical instruments and medical testing equipment. The sterile room reminded her of the clinic room they had strapped her down in when she had been taken against her will. It scared her, but she focused on the doctor and trying to reach him.

"I'm way too smart for you, little Abigail," he taunted.

Refusing to be daunted by the truth in his words, Abby set her face into a scowl and struggled harder to reach out for him.

"You're never going to catch me," he jeered.

His words, the clear mocking in his tone coupled with his smug sense of superiority inflamed her anger—and simultaneously her sense of being inferior—further.

Struggling for breath, she tried harder. The more she tried, the more he seemed to slip from her reach.

He stepped back from her and she noticed now they were in his medical office, the rooms he had used to consult in where she had first met him before this nightmare had begun. His desk had papers piled all over it, reports and graphs, diagrams and journals scattered one on top of the other until a veritable mini-mountain had been created.

That struck her as strange, unlike how she recalled his desk, but the feeling passed fleetingly as she saw his degrees, diplomas and various accreditation certificates in their matching wooden frames. The only certificate in a different, plastic, frame appeared old and faded. It was a certificate of thanks for 'continual support' from a nursing home. That particular item had always struck her as odd. Continual support of any style seemed very unlike the cool, detached doctor she had seen at each of her appointments, as did his having placed it on his ego wall.

"I'm going to kill you, just as I killed all those other people," Harper said, drawing her attention back to him once again.

Abigail tried to turn away, to ignore the words he'd spat at her, but she found herself helpless, unable to move yet again.

Panic flared in her anew. Confronting Paul Harper was scary. She had known that from the moment she'd decided to do so. With Lucas by her side, watching over her, touching her, casting that wicked, lovely smile at her she could ignore the fear that always seemed to bubble beneath the surface. She could rise above it.

Here, alone, she struggled with the darkness of doubt and worry as it slowly blossomed into terror.

The realisation she was trapped almost undid her.

"Don't," she pleaded as Harper came closer to her with a syringe filled with clear fluid.

"This is your iron injection, Abigail," he crooned. "You don't want to get sick, do you?"

"Please," she cried out. "Don't."

"Now, now." The doctor tutted. "If you don't take this like a good girl I might give it to Lucas. I'd love to poison him. You wouldn't want that, would you?"

"No!" she cried out, petrified.

"I thought not." The doctor smirked as he continued to advance upon her.

Abigail twisted and turned desperately, but her arms and legs were held fast. There was no way out.

"I'll kill Lucas slowly, just as I am killing you, even now. Then I can move onto Tristan and Kimber, everyone you know and care for will slowly be eaten away from the inside, just like what is happening to you, Abigail."

"Stop it! Let me go! Help!" Abby screamed.

"Abby, Abby, Abby," Harper repeated her name over and over and over until she wanted to block her ears. He didn't let up, though, repeating her name until she finally managed somehow to break free of his hold.

She tripped on something – she had no idea what it was – then she fell and continued to fall forever…

* * *

Warm arms caught her, snapping her out of the dream and back into reality. For one wild, terrorising moment Abigail thought she was back in the clinic, restrained to the bed. She was reliving the nightmare.

"Abby, darling, wake up, please!" Lucas urged her, true fear in his tone.

Abby twisted around, turning into him to gaze in his eyes, needing to reassure herself he was there, real and she was awake and not still sleeping.

"Lucas?" Her voice trembled with her need for this to be true. She reached up and he let her shoulders go. Patiently, he allowed her to touch his jaw, to trace her fingers over his lips then stroke his cheek as she tried to catch her breath.

"I dreamt…Harper was saying… Oh Lucas, I'm not sure I'm strong enough for this after all," she stammered, barely able to finish one thought before another came crashing over it.

"Give it time, Abby," Lucas soothed. This time when he wrapped an arm around her shoulders she scooted closer to him on the tiny cot bed and huddled in the warmth of his embrace, relieved beyond measure he was here for her right now.

She didn't recall falling asleep. The last thing she remembered was being at the desk, searching through so many papers and her eyes drooping. Lucas must have carried her there. Peeking out over his arms, she saw lockers at the far end of the room, a person-high privacy screen cordoning off this area and a handful of cot beds, all empty except for the one they currently used.

Her heart beating wildly, Abigail buried her head in Lucas' shoulder and calmed her breathing, soaking up the warmth of his body. Never had she been so grateful for another person's presence. He stroked her hair, the smooth motion acting like the most wonderful balm to her senses. His touch as much as the rhythm of his actions eased her back into reality and far away from her horrid remembrance of Harper.

"He said he was killing me slowly," she mumbled against Lucas' shoulder, moving closer to him until she sat between his spread legs. "He said he needed to inject me again, that if I didn't let him he'd poison you. I couldn't let him do it, I just couldn't."

"Hey"—Lucas hushed her with a kiss to her forehead—"Harper isn't getting near you, with or without a syringe. And I dare the bastard to try to poison me. That would require him getting close enough for me to break every tooth in his mouth then ram them down his throat."

Abigail smiled a little wanly at the mental image this brought up. She lifted her head to gaze adoringly at Lucas. She sighed, her heartbeat finally settling. Cupping his jaw in her hands she kissed him slowly, thoroughly.

Exploring his lips and mouth with her tongue, she parried an intimate duel with him, her eagerness growing as her pussy became damp. She sucked his tongue fully into her mouth. Lucas stroked her back. She shivered at the enticing sensation. After raising herself up, she moved her thighs so that she straddled him.

She lifted her fingers to the top button on his shirt and quickly unfastened it. Her breaths came faster as her heart pounded. Heat flooded her body and she couldn't deny the intoxicating effect this man had on her every sense. Abby craved him more and more each moment. Lucas was like an exotic drug, addictive and going straight to her head.

"Abby, I don't think—"

"I want to," she interrupted him. "No one else is in this early, are they?"

"Only a few from the graveyard shift," he replied. "Tristan and Kimber are bunked down in the main medical area. The beds there are way more comfortable. I didn't think you'd want to wake up there, with the hospital smells and instruments after…well, I didn't think you'd like that."

"Then this is the perfect opportunity," she responded, kissing him hard. The fact he'd been so thoughtful, even to the obvious detriment of his own comfort, had her chest heating with more love for him.

Lucas was her hero in every respect.

"I want you, right now." She peppered kisses down his neck as they both tugged his shirt off. "I don't want to wait for some mythical perfect time, or until we've had a chance to exchange all our secrets. I know everything I need to know about you already. You're kind, you're thoughtful and have a good soul."

"You're giving me a big head." He chuckled while she set to work at his belt and waistband.

Abigail giggled and pressed her hand teasingly against the rock-hard length of his shaft.

"I'll say it's big," she said with a wicked wink.

Lucas groaned.

Abigail eased herself down from the cot so that she knelt between his legs. She looked up at him, holding his hot blue gaze in her own. With his help she had him stripped naked in seconds. Licking and kissing his soft, exposed skin she meandered her way down his chest. They both laughed as he forced her to pause here and there while he tugged her T-shirt off up over her head.

Lucas exposed her dark green, lacy bra. He fondled her breasts through the scrap with evident relish. Tingles raced over her skin and her nipples beaded, scraping enticingly along the sheer material. Abby bent her head and licked the tip of his heated cock.

His bulbous head was slick with the juices of his pre-cum. When she intimately tasted his salty, musky flavour she mumbled with pleasure. Running her tongue over him repeatedly she sucked the length of his cock down her throat. The faster she moved the harsher his pants came. Lucas canted his hips up into her ministrations.

As he threaded his hand across the back of her scalp, tiny thrills of pleasure sparked along the line his touch had left. She shuddered in response, craving everything she could experience with him. He clasped his fingers in her long hair and guided her head farther down his long stalk.

Eager to comply, Abigail opened her mouth until she buried her lips into the crinkled hairs against his skin and the tip of his head bumped into the back of her throat.

"Fuck yes," he panted, clearly lost in sensations.

Abigail bobbed her head once slowly, testing whether she could manage and finding that she enjoyed the feel of him. She breathed carefully and repeated the gesture.

Over and over she lifted and lowered her lips, laving her tongue along the thickness of his cock.

Lucas groaned, the sound almost as if he were in pain. She did it again, thrilled at the power she felt and the pleasure she could give him.

Lucas panted in earnest and she could see the trembling in his upper thighs as he struggled to retain his control. Working into a faster momentum, she really began to enjoy herself when he tilted his hips high, pressing his cock deeper down her throat. It took her a moment for her to become comfortable with his size and relax her muscles so she'd not gag. After she'd adjusted she tried to swallow down around him, humming to add a slight vibration to the sensations she could inflict upon his hardness.

"Fuck, oh yes, Abby," he moaned eagerly. He clutched his hand at her head, dragging her lower upon him. The head of his erection started to resonate and she tasted the saltiness of his pre-cum as he reached his limits.

"I'm going to come, darling," he panted.

Abigail lifted her eyes and saw with surprise he watched her intently, his gaze burning with intensity. She continued to bob her head, sucking him as hard as she could while stroking his shaft with her tongue in continual strokes.

"Last chance," he whispered.

She watched when he shuddered, biting his lips to stifle his groans of release.

His shaft plunged deeper inside her throat and erupted. Splashes of seed filled her mouth and she swallowed convulsively. Sucking on him, she worked her throat and drank his seed, pleased to smell their mingled scents as he ejaculated.

When there was nothing left to swallow, Abigail was surprised to realise he was still quite hard within her. Tenderly touching him, she discovered he had wilted somewhat, but still remained partially erect.

Lucas cupped her face and drew her up and off him.

"Oh no, my naughty minx," he whispered huskily as he guided her up onto the cot next to him. "If you keep on doing that we're just going to have an encore exactly the same as what I just enjoyed."

"I liked sucking you off," she replied. Her smile was wide and warm, she was pleased with herself and feeling faintly smug.

She let Lucas press her down onto the bed and helped him to remove her bra, jeans and knickers. Lucas kissed her lips, easing his tongue inside her to taste himself.

"Mmm," he muttered, clearly enjoying it. "I've been craving to taste you since I first saw your photo. If we're going to do this then I want to give as good as I get, love."

Ducking his head, he took her nipple into his mouth, sucking on it and causing her to arch up in pleasure. Spreading her legs wide apart as he nudged her, Abigail let Lucas settle himself between her shivering thighs. He ran his thick fingers through the slick lips of her pussy.

Finding her clit with devastating skill, he then swirled some cream around her entrance, lubricating her. Sensations beat at her with overwhelming intensity. She felt his touch as if he shot electricity over her. Her nipples, stomach, back, neck and even her toes hummed with power and need, seemingly connected as the pleasure rode her hard. Lifting herself up into Lucas' embrace, Abby moaned wantonly.

"Please," she begged him, needing to feel his thickness possessing her.

Lucas nipped a stinging kiss on the sensitive spot under the curve of her breast.

"Patience," he purred.

Abigail reached her hand down to cup his heated sac, circling two fingers around the root of his shaft.

"Now, please. I need to feel you inside me. I want you to fuck me so badly, Lucas. I can't possibly be patient."

Groaning, Lucas lowered himself until his mouth covered her leaking pussy. He lapped at her, drinking her down. She placed the back of her hand to her mouth to stop the scream of satisfaction that threatened to escape. Riding high on need, she ached. His every action thrilled her — but still she wanted more.

Lucas thrust his tongue deeply, licking at her inner walls and filling her in an erotic mockery of what they both craved.

Stroking her nipples with the tips of his fingers, Lucas then pinched and squeezed her lightly. This served to keep her panting and wanting to beg for more. She tilted her hips up, eager for more of his touch. Lucas licked her thoroughly, suckling her clit, then returning to stroke her labia. He nipped his teeth lightly at her swollen folds.

Higher and higher he drove her, need twisting within her stomach until she felt certain she would explode. Yet the more he gave her the more she seemed able to take, soaking up his every caress like a sponge.

Abigail cried with dismay when he removed one of his hands from her breasts to grope on the floor for his pants. She heard a crinkle as he withdrew a small packet. Lucas lifted himself above her, rising like some devastatingly handsome ancient warrior, ready to plunder his conquest. Willingly, she spread herself wider open and helped guide him inside her body.

Both of them panted with need as he slid his cock into her body. Despite dripping with ardent desire, she struggled to encompass his width. Easing himself in and out, Lucas slowly brought their bodies together. Abigail lifted her hips to assist his possession of her. She cried out when he plunged deeply into her. Finally the feel of having him fill her, penetrate her to his root drove her wild with desire.

"Hush, darling," Lucas whispered, lowering himself over her so they could press their lips together. Kissing her reverently, he remained enveloped fully within her tight passage.

"I couldn't stop now, not even if every member of the Agency broke in through that door, but let's not invite them just yet," he cautioned her.

"Then give me something else to do with my mouth," she teased.

They kissed with an intensity she could never have believed existed. Lucas rocked within her, slowly at first but soon gathering speed as they both lost all sense of control. Abby grabbed hold of his back, moving her hands against his sweat-coated skin. She dug her short nails in for purchase and when he grunted she had to loosen her grip.

Lucas lifted his hands under her thighs, opening her wider and shifted her hips so that he could plunge even deeper. Abigail tightened her inner muscles, squeezing down and around him. The extra pressure sent her over the edge. Like the detonation of a bomb blast, her orgasm rocked her. Pleasure vibrated through her pussy, her nipples and her stomach as she screamed into his mouth and he swallowed her climax.

Instantly the tighter contractions ripped his orgasm from him. Lucas came with a muffled roar, thrusting hard and fierce into her as he rode through his second, and much longer, release. Abigail's muscles spasmed and twitched as she collapsed back against the cot bed, the thin frame shuddering threateningly from the rough treatment.

It remained steady, though Abby realised they both held themselves carefully as if awaiting the structure to fold in on itself. Lucas huffed out a few barely suppressed chuckles.

"That would have sucked if the bed had broken," he joked. "Talk about mood ruiner. And then we would have had to somehow dispose of the frame because – well how could we have possibly explained?"

Abigail wiped the sweat from her brow and reached for her lover. He pulled his cock from her, bent to quickly kiss her lips then stood up and crossed to the tiny sink in the far corner.

Turning onto her side, Abby watched him with interest as he tidied himself. Lucas gathered a wad of paper towels and wet them before bringing them to her. Standing on shaking legs, she paused a moment to get her bearings, then carefully walked over to the basin to clean herself up. After doing the best she could, Abigail returned to their cot. Pulling on her knickers and T-shirt she dressed with care, not wanting to appear overly rumbled or as debauched as she felt. When she finished, she settled back on the cot. Lucas, wearing only his boxers, tugged her down into a spooning position.

Knowing all too soon they would have to get up, dress and get back to the mountain of paperwork, Abigail just enjoyed the tender moment they shared. Her mind wandered, then she recalled the papers, prodding her brain back into the dream. Feeling lazy and sated while the musings of Dr Harper and his poisonous words still made her feel faintly ill, something niggled urgently in the back of her head.

Frowning, she tried to bring the entire dream into focus, the fear and desperation she had felt making her shiver.

"What is it, darling?" Lucas asked, his voice filled with concern.

She shook her head but decided speaking of it might help the dream lose its sting.

"That dream I had, the one you woke me from. Something about it is pricking my memory."

"Don't worry about it," Lucas insisted. "I wasn't just placating you. I meant it. I won't let Dr Harper hurt you. I swear."

Abigail turned over in the slender cot. Lucas wrapped his arms around her as they shared the pillow and she held him tightly around the waist.

"I know," she replied. She looked at him a moment, drinking in how this handsome man held her and made the world feel so much brighter. She smiled warmly at him. "I believe you, fully. That's not it. I was thinking of the paperwork we have waiting for us, and that reminded me that in the dream Dr Harper's desk was literally piled with papers. It struck me as not right in the dream and I almost pulled out of it then, but his ego wall—all those diplomas and certificates and accreditation whatnots—that was all right and real and dragged me back in."

"I don't follow." Lucas frowned.

Abigail realised he'd genuinely listened and wanted her to explain so he could follow her train of thought.

"Something about that part of the dream is pulling on my memory, like it's important."

"Okay then, describe it all to me, everything you can remember. Walking through it slowly and in such detail might jog loose whatever your subconscious is telling you."

Abigail described Harper's desk in as much detail as she could manage. When she finished she shook her head with frustration.

"That can't be it then," Lucas said with seemingly infinite patience. "Describe his ego wall now."

"Maybe I'm making too much of it," she sighed.

Lucas stroked her hair tenderly.

"No, darling, we have as long as it takes. Now describe the ego wall for me. You said there were his diplomas?"

"Yeah, a whole slew of certificates of different courses he had completed."

"Okay then, list those you can for me. And the other things you mentioned, his accreditations I think you said. Oh, and the certificates of thanks, too."

Abigail frowned, a tiny frisson of energy racing through her at his words. It jogged a memory right on the tip of her tongue. Lucas leant back and she basked at having his heated gaze upon her. She remained silent, mentally clutching for the knowledge she could feel just barely out of reach.

"The certificate of thanks," she said after some thought, afraid if she pushed it would disappear on her. "It was different from the others. All the other frames were matching, as if he'd bought them in bulk or done them all up prettily at the same time. But the certificate, that was different. A plastic frame. Older than the others, worn and faded."

Lucas remained silent, but the air crackled with the weight of his awareness. It snapped like a living thing between them. She knew he hung on her every word but would wait until she had grasped what eluded her, instead of ploughing ahead or interrupting her train of thought.

"It read—'With thanks to Doctor Paul Harper for his Continual Support to the Highvale Nursing Home, London'."

Pride surged through her and she grinned, pleased she'd managed to recall the detail. Lifting her eyes to Lucas, excitement hummed over her skin. She sat up, eager.

"There can't be too many Highvale nursing homes in London, surely?" She felt hopeful.

"I wouldn't think so," Lucas replied slowly. He sat and rubbed a hand through his hair.

Abby held her breath, waiting expectantly for him to tell her what utter rubbish this was. He kept silent for a brief moment, then a smile spread over his face.

"It can't possibly hurt to look. I know this is just a dream of yours. It's only a possibility that it stems from a real memory, but you spent time in his office.

It's crazy, undoubtedly, but it's still something we can move on."

"It's not like I expect he's out there right now, hiding out among the retired folks," she agreed. "But it's a connection he has no reason to suspect anyone knows about."

Lucas nodded and drew her in for a quick kiss.

"You're brilliant, you know that?"

Excited, they both rushed off the small bed and hastened to get dressed.

Chapter Five

"Thank you very much," Abby said before hanging up the phone. She scrawled down the number for the Highvale Nursing Home. It was just past dawn and despite the fact she'd had almost no sleep and by rights she should be exhausted, the thrill of success sent adrenaline through her body.

"I've got it!" she cheered, feeling exultant and beaming at Lucas, who said a hasty "Never mind" and hung up his phone. He whooped, raced towards her and gave her an enormous kiss. Throwing her arms around him, she eagerly returned the embrace, laughing.

"Did we miss the party?" Tristan interjected.

Abigail beamed, not upset in the least they'd chosen this moment to return. Kimber's blonde curls sprung up all around her head, clearly mussed from the few hours' sleep they'd managed to get. She looked tired but intrigued by the obvious excitement. It was a very different atmosphere to when they'd left earlier.

"Not yet, mate," Lucas replied eagerly. "But if you'd slept much longer you might have."

"You got a break in the case and didn't wake me?" Tristan said, clearly unhappy.

"No, not really," Abigail insisted. "I woke up from a nightmare, one involving Dr Harper. I knew there was something in it my subconscious was trying to remind me, but it took me a little bit to work out."

Abigail glanced from Tristan to Kimber, to Lucas and back to Tristan again as she tried to explain and settle Tristan's understandably ruffled feathers.

"He had a certificate of thanks hung up in his office. It was from the Highvale Nursing Home. It's probably nothing at all, another dead end, but the certificate was in commemoration of 'continual support' which he'd given them."

"Do you really remember that? Or has the dream twisted something to make it appear like that?" Tristan asked. His tone suggested curiosity, not disbelief.

"I know a certificate really was on his wall," Abby replied firmly. "Whether it honestly said Highvale Nursing Home or not I can't swear to. It's been a while and I wasn't making notes, so I can only work with what the memory of my dream was."

"That's fair enough," Tristan replied. "So you've called around and confirmed this home exists?"

"Yep." Abigail smiled and waved her ripped sheet of notebook paper.

"It's a long shot, mate," Lucas concluded. "Abby and I figured I'd call them, act like a patient—or more likely a colleague—who really needed to contact Harper and dig around for a further lead. If it had paid off I would have woken you then. I didn't relish the thought of waking you before we knew if this would lead somewhere, especially when you and Kimber have barely had a couple of hours sleep. I also figured had the positions been reversed and you were chasing a very long shot by making a few calls you'd have not woken me, either."

Tristan appeared struck by this thought. He chewed it over for a moment before agreeing.

"Fair point," he conceded.

Abigail shot a look to Lucas, asking with her eyes if she should give him the number. Lucas tilted his head to Tristan and she nodded.

She held the slip of paper silently out to Tristan, who shook his head.

"No, this was your idea," he said graciously. "Let Lucas finish it. He's right, a few phone calls to follow a wild hunch is not something to get myself upset over. You both did the right thing in not sitting around letting it get cold. Besides, Kimber and I are here now, so we're not missing out."

Lucas took the number from Abigail's fingers and sat on the edge of the desk she had been using. After pressing the numbers in quick succession, he turned to face the three of them as the phone rang.

"Yes, I'd like to speak to the nurse in charge of the shift please," Lucas said into the phone. "Of course."

Covering the mouthpiece, he mouthed, "On hold" to them. Abigail struggled to not wriggle with impatience. She felt deep in her gut as if they were close to tracking Dr Harper down now—she only hoped she hadn't let her expectations and hopes blind her to the reality.

Before she could really work herself up into a state over anything, Lucas snapped back to attention on the phone.

"Yes, madam, thank you for answering so promptly. I'm hoping this is a very simple question. I'm looking to get in touch with Dr Paul Harper. We've been working together on a project lately and he hasn't answered my calls for most of the last week. I've made numerous calls to his home and work with no success. He's mentioned in the past his great works with your home and I was hoping you might be able to assist me."

Abigail leaned closer to hear the nurse's side of the conversation as best she could. It wasn't perfect, but she understood enough to follow.

"Yes, of course. Paul has been instrumental in assisting our residents with their...such a fine man. He was tireless in...with his mother, the Lord rest her soul. We haven't seen...she passed away, oh it must be almost six months ago. He is supposed to come vaccinate the residents with their annual flu shots later in the week. I spoke to him only the other day..."

"Really, the other day, you say? How wonderful. And he is supposed to come by later in the week? I wonder if he's made a firm commitment with you? An exact time and date? I would dearly love to catch up with him."

At Lucas' words Tristan stood straighter, an eager gleam in his eye. He reminded Abigail of a hawk who had spotted his prey but was as yet unable to make the kill, circling patiently but extremely aware of every nuance.

"Why no, I'm afraid he hasn't."

"Would you happen to have a number I could contact him on?" Lucas asked as he scrambled around the desk, picking up the summary sheet they'd been using. "I'm afraid the number I have doesn't seem to be connecting." Lucas recited the number they had for Harper's home line, which now tapped and appeared abandoned.

"Oh dear, that's the number we...can't think how we can contact him. Unless, well yes, he might be staying at his mother's old house in Stockwell."

"Stockwell?" Lucas repeated. Tristan snapped to attention, tossing Lucas a notebook and pen before crossing to the nearest desk. Bending over, he booted up the computer sitting there. Abigail continued to listen in on the phone conversation as Tristan typed in a series of commands on the computer.

"Why yes, actually it makes sense now, for…set up a lab there…years ago. Back when he grew up there it wasn't such a good area, of course…glad he'd held onto it for with the basement lab it's worth quite a pretty penny nowadays. He told me…the flu shots and that he should be ready with them by the end of the week and I told him… So that must be where he's gone off to."

"I don't suppose you'd have the address or phone number of his mother's old house would you? It would really be perfect if I could call him so we could wrap this project up."

"I'm sure I have it around here somewhere, let me just…"

Lucas wrote in the notebook, Abigail reading the address and phone number with a growing sense of excitement. Lucas caught her gaze and returned it with a satisfied smirk when he'd finished, passing her the pad and indicating with a tilt of his chin to pass it over to Tristan. She got up and walked the notebook to him.

Tristan had opened a few tabs full of different search engines and logged onto his internal email. Already he had typed up a brief summary to be sent to Preston Jones, presumably before they left. Tristan acknowledged the data with a silent nod, speedily typing it into the text of the email with an update of what they had discovered and the process they'd followed to retrieve it.

"You've been a marvellous help, Henriette, thank you so much," Lucas said before he hung up the phone. "You emailing Jones?" Lucas asked.

"Yep, right now. Do you want to call and leave a message that we'll be taking a kit each and a pool car? The guys down in the equipment store get twitchy when people just lift their gear without letting them know," Tristan said while typing on the keyboard.

"I need another clip of ammo and I've left my cuffs at my flat," Lucas said. "Otherwise I should be all right with what I have in my duffel. You?"

"I never leave my cuffs at my place," Tristan replied with a grin. "I don't want to know why you took yours home with you."

"Hey, none of that!" Lucas snapped though there was no real heat to his tone. Tristan cast a quick look of apology towards Abigail and changed the topic.

"Make sure you get a car that we can contain him in. One of us will drive and the other can sit in back with him when we return and —"

"Hang on, we're coming too, right?" Kimber interrupted for the first time, a frown gathering on her brow. The blonde looked to Abigail for support and received it.

"Absolutely. It was my dream — or idea at least — that got us here. I don't want to sit here twiddling my thumbs waiting for you manly men to bring the bad bloke home. That's not at all fair," she replied firmly.

"And you'd be absolutely nowhere on these vaccines nor have found Abigail in the first place without me," Kimber added.

Tristan and Lucas exchanged speaking glances.

"Hey." Abigail nudged Lucas. "Don't do that."

"Tristan, I really think that —" Kimber talked softly to Tristan.

Abigail used the opportunity to take a moment with Lucas semi-privately.

"You really can't be serious," she said in a low tone, but the weight of her frustration could be heard.

Lucas looked uncomfortable as they turned fully towards each other. "I don't like the thought of you being in danger, Abby," he confessed. "This could backfire—an assault on his home! I couldn't live with myself if you were hurt. You've been through enough, darling."

Much of Abigail's anger melted at his words, but she remained firm.

"It's my decision whether I put myself in danger, Lucas," she sighed. "I love it that you want to protect me, and I get thrills just from the obvious ways you show how much you care about me. But I need to see this through to the end. I want to be there when you and Tristan arrest his arse and throw him unwillingly in the back seat of your car."

"Justice?" Lucas guessed.

"And vengeance," she admitted a little sheepishly. "The mental picture of him being carted away goes a long way to soothing my hurt and upset at what he put me through. It doesn't take it away or make it better, but it certainly helps."

Lucas studied her for a moment and she met his gaze as calmly as she could manage. She refused to resort to threats or ultimatums, they would only antagonise him and belittle what she felt was her genuine right to be present.

Sure, she had read the address and knew roughly where it was. Five minutes with a map and she could drive herself there. But that would be deceitful and worse, it would effectively force Lucas' hand. Abigail wanted him to come to the decision himself, not because she bullied him into it.

"...you know I'm right." Abigail heard Kimber finish passionately.

Tristan sighed.

The two agents exchanged another look.

"They could take a separate car," Lucas suggested, whether to his partner or Abigail she didn't know.

"We could still take him into custody and drive him back safely, the girls can watch from outside, out of danger," Tristan seemed to agree reluctantly.

"Would that be a fair compromise?" Lucas asked with a brief glance towards Kimber.

She felt a weight in his glance as his eyes settled back on her. Lucas waited for Abigail's response. She thought for a second before agreeing. It did seem like a fair middle ground to her. She'd still be able to watch and see for herself Harper being stopped, but she knew Lucas would be more at ease with her out of the way of immediate danger.

"I'm happy with that," she replied. She turned and glanced at Kimber, who nodded her assent.

Tristan picked up the phone and dialled a few digits.

"Let me organise the cars, then we can get our kits," he said. "I want to get this done as soon as possible. The later into the morning we leave it the higher the chance he'll have a chance to escape."

"I need you to swear to me you'll stay well back," Lucas said as he wrapped Abigail up in a tight hug.

She pulled him close, settling her arms around his slender waist easily, as if they had been doing this for years and not a few days.

"I'm not looking for trouble here," she said, the sound muffled into the warmth of his chest. "You're the hero. I haven't forgotten that at all. I am more than prepared to sit back and just watch the show. I'm not looking for glory. I just want to see Dr Harper brought in. I promise."

"Part of me worries I won't be able to focus with you there, Abby. The thought of you in danger, or possibly being hurt, it messes with my head."

She lifted her gaze and caught his burning look. Rising onto tiptoes she steadied herself with a hand to his arm. Abigail kissed Lucas hard, a promise embedded in the affection.

"I'll stay out on the footpath, well out of the way of trouble. Don't worry about me, please. I'd hate to think you were focused on me and not Harper and the job you were doing."

Lucas rubbed his hand up and down her back. Love rose in her chest for this man. Even when he was annoyed or frustrated, he still showed her in many little ways how deeply he cared. Tingles shivered over her skin at the contact.

"How about we have a late breakfast—or possibly lunch—at my place after this is all over?" she offered.

Lucas grinned, clearly pleased with the idea.

"What? Like a real date or something? Would we even know what to do?"

"We can muddle through it, I'm sure," she said, then laughed a little nervously. The mood lightened, and with a final, gentle squeeze they separated once again.

Tristan whispered a few more words to Kimber and kissed her forehead. With a tilt of his head Tristan indicated for Lucas to follow him.

"Let's go and get our kits organised. Kimber, you and Abby can go and pick up the keys to the cars from the equipment area and meet us back here. We shouldn't be too long."

An edgy kind of excitement rolled in her stomach. She would not have missed this for anything, but she couldn't deny the fact that she felt grateful she'd merely be a bystander and Lucas would be the one with the difficult task of bringing Harper in.

She prayed it would all go smoothly.

* * * *

Abigail's phone rang, startling her as Kimber drove.

"Is that the blokes?" Kimber asked when she glanced away from the road.

"I have no idea," Abby replied, curious.

They'd been following Tristan and Lucas only for about five minutes and still had them in sight. She couldn't think of a reason for them to be calling at this early stage.

"Maybe they forgot something and needed to turn around?" Kimber postulated.

Abigail wriggled in her seat, the belt restricting her movements and making digging the phone out of her pocket difficult.

"I'd have thought they'd just turn around if that was the case." Abigail grunted as she got a grip on the small mobile and tugged it free. "We're following them, after all. If they—oh, I don't recognise the number."

Curious and only a little nervous she pressed the 'receive' button.

"Hello?"

"Yes, I'd like to speak to Miss Abigail Turner, please, it's Dr Morrison."

Kimber had tilted her head towards Abby, clearly puzzled, though she continued to drive.

"Dr Morrison, this is Abby, what can I do for you?" Abigail wondered for a moment if the doctor had spent the entire night working in the lab. She felt a bit bad at the thought.

"I have your results here, are you still in the building? I tried calling Sloan's desk but only got his voicemail."

Dr Morrison's words had her stomach tightening. In a flash Abby knew she didn't really want to know if there was something wrong with her after all.

For the first time in years she felt content, as if she were exactly where she was meant to be. It didn't matter her feelings for Lucas were brand-new, they were important to her and he was quickly becoming her entire world. If some useless medical reports were going to tear that world apart she wasn't certain she wanted to know it at all.

Abigail licked her lips and cast a glance at Kimber, who stared firmly ahead at the road and tried to pretend she couldn't hear what went on. Abigail sighed. No matter how deeply she thrust her head in the proverbial sand it wouldn't make anything bad go away. She didn't believe Lucas would leave her if Dr Morrison had bad news for her, but she had also promised herself not many hours ago she would no longer act cowardly or let things beyond her control affect her actions.

She might as well hear what the doctor had to say, listen to his advice and make her own decisions, preferably after a private talk with Lucas, if it came to that.

"Kimber, Tristan, Lucas and I are en route to hopefully collect Dr Harper," she explained. "I'm grateful you obviously stayed through the night to get these results promptly, Dr Morrison. That means a lot to me."

"I'd have done the same for anyone in these circumstances," the doctor replied gruffly.

Abigail smiled. She genuinely liked the elderly man.

"I still truly appreciate it. Now, please, give me the news before I have a heart attack because my imagination is running overtime."

"Actually there isn't anything for you to get upset about," Morrison replied. She heard papers rustling on his end of the phone. "We found no significant evidence of the various diseases Kimber warned us about, though a few of the less common natural bacteria one finds in the human body were found in higher levels than I would expect. Also your white blood cell count is extremely high—but that could indicate you had recently fought off anything as minor as a cold or as serious as influenza. It's impossible to tell."

"So what does that mean?" Abigail glanced outside the window and tried to assemble her thoughts and grasp the deeper meaning.

"At face value, my dear, it means you're perfectly healthy."

Abigail wrinkled her nose.

"And underneath that?"

"I'd hate to postulate," Morrison hedged.

"Then just between you and me? Not in an official report."

Morrison was silent for a moment. She heard the sound of a door closing and his chair squeak as he presumably sat back down.

"Privately, Abigail, I would think only one of a few things could have occurred. Either Dr Harper's vaccine did indeed boost your immune system and cause your body to overcome a range of pathogens that we believe killed those other people. Or possibly you simply have a very strong, robust and natural immunity to most diseases—some people do, you know. Or a far more remote possibility is that Kimberly's sample was contaminated, or a mix up or other form of error occurred on the initial testing."

"Okay," she replied slowly as she thought it through. Abigail now understood why Dr Morrison was not keen to express his thoughts too loudly as yet. It could be potentially explosive, and for her at least, life altering.

"What will you do now?" she asked.

"You said you were en route to find Dr Harper?" Morrison asked.

Abigail agreed.

"Then I believe I will lock these results away in my private drawer, grab a few hours' sleep and see how events unfold. There's no need for me to make my report or a recommendation immediately. Indeed, no one here even knows I've completed the tests."

Without clearly stating so, Abigail gathered what the doctor offered her. He gave the four of them time. They could hopefully find Harper, get him in custody. If they could make him explain what he had done, perhaps even why and what he'd wanted to achieve it could answer their questions.

Morrison appeared as if he were willing to give them space and make a plan of action. She grinned, relieved and grateful for his flexibility.

"That would be fantastic, thank you. I promise to call you back when we have some answers to share. Will you be available on this number?"

"Certainly. Good luck, Abigail."

"Thank you very much, Dr Morrison."

Abigail disconnected the phone, feeling a lot lighter than she had in a while. The weight she'd been carrying unconsciously since learning of Harper's experiments on her and their devastating consequences to his other 'patients' had not evaporated completely. There was still a lot she didn't understand.

"Is everything all right?" Kimber asked tentatively.

Abigail took a deep breath. She pushed her phone back in her pocket.

"Dr Morrison didn't find anything wrong with me," she replied.

Kimber remained silent, clearly thinking this information through.

"Well, that's good news then?" Kimber finally said, a lilt at the end of her sentence clearly making the statement a question.

Abigail nibbled on her lower lip before she consciously stopped the nervous gesture.

"I feel perfectly fine. If Dr Morrison says there's nothing showing up in my blood work, that's what I should focus on, right?"

"Definitely," Kimber agreed.

They drove in silence, both seeming lost in their own thoughts.

"Should I be worried?" Abby heard herself say, despite her desire to leave it and change the topic.

They paused at a light and Kimber seemed to study her a minute.

When the light changed they continued and Kimber replied, "I guess that depends on what you want to do. Are you interested in starting some legitimate research into what effect the vaccine has had on you? You need to think carefully about that, because once the door's open you can't close it again."

"I might not have a choice," Abby pointed out. "Harper's research is out there, we have no real idea of whether he's spread it around, or got silent partners, or even if he's stashed his notes and samples in a dozen different places."

Her tone rose as she became stressed at the number of aspects she didn't have control over. Abigail paused to take a deep breath.

"Let's try this instead," Kimber urged in a soothing tone. "With what we have now, ignoring all the things

Dr Harper might or might not have done, what do you want?"

"I'd move on with my life," she replied simply. "I want to explore a relationship with Lucas, lead a normal existence. I don't want people poking and prodding me, testing vaccinations out on me or analysing my blood or immune system for years on end."

"I doubt any laboratory would get official permission to do so," Kimber said. "But if that's what you want, then you should aim for it."

"Act if it's the truth and that will convince everyone it is?" Abigail replied with a wry humour.

"It can't hurt, especially for now."

"I'll need to deal with Harper and his notes, studies and who knows what else rather soon though, won't I?"

"I'm not so sure. Lucas seems utterly smitten with you, and Tristan values him as a partner," Kimberly confided. "You might find the men will figure out a way to protect you."

"Dr Morrison has already helped in that respect. He's not going to write up his report until we've spoken with Dr Harper."

"It will work out," Kimber insisted optimistically.

Abigail smiled, though it felt lacklustre at best.

Chapter Six

Lucas and Tristan had discussed at length in the car whether they would use stealth to enter Dr Harper's residence or just crash in with guns blazing. Back and forth they had debated the pros and cons of each attempt, frequently playing the devil's advocate merely to flesh out each possible scenario.

Eventually they had agreed to remain discreet and keep a low profile out in the street, but break down any doors and barriers to gain admittance to and within the house. Lucas worried they had both avoided the topic of what to do with what they would find. He had been about to raise the topic as they parked, but the girls were right behind them and the moment had been lost.

"We need you girls to stay back here with the cars no matter what," Lucas said, giving Abby a hard look.

"I don't like the way that sounds," Kimber protested.

Tristan touched her shoulder.

"You promised to stay out of the way," he reminded her. "Harper is only a dozen houses down this street.

If we park any closer he'll see us and we will lose the element of surprise."

"We have to get moving or the street will fill up. Everyone will be leaving for work shortly, so our window of opportunity is getting narrow. Please, Abby, Kimber, just stay in the car," Lucas requested.

Both girls agreed and climbed back into their car, though Lucas noticed they both craned their necks to catch sight of the house he had indicated.

"Ready?" he asked Tristan.

His partner nodded.

Both men crossed the street and walked at a normal pace towards Dr Harper's mother's house. As they got closer Lucas counted ahead and saw its front garden was overgrown with dead and dying weeds, the door and frame dilapidated and painted a faded blue.

"The blue one," Tristan said, clearly echoing his thoughts.

"Got it," Lucas replied as they walked. "Should we circle around and see if there's a back entrance, or just go straight through the front?"

"I haven't seen a single person out on the street as yet," Tristan spoke quickly—they were only a few doors away from their target. "You'd think at this hour people would be walking the dog or going for a run, it's an hour past dawn. We'll gather more attention from coming back so soon, there's not exactly a crowd to blend into."

"Agreed," Lucas replied. "I say we take our chances with breaking down the door. If we do it with one hit, smooth, quick and close it behind us it could be a few minutes before anyone works out what we've done."

"Hell, if we do it like that people might not notice at all. It's too early for the neighbours to be in the front of their homes, close enough to hear and be peeking out of the curtains. We should both shoulder it open together and to hell with what the neighbours might hear."

"Sounds like a plan," Lucas agreed as without missing a beat they both ascended the stairs.

As if choreographed they continued to walk at a steady pace directly up to the front door and with a simultaneous "Three" they forced their weight behind their shoulders, the splintering crack of wood the only sound rending the air.

Lucas felt a dull ache in his shoulder but he easily pushed it aside to focus on the task at hand. Tristan entered the hallway first, Lucas following. They pulled their guns out. Lucas grunted as he shoved the door back into its place as best he could. Tristan held up a hand, his head cocked.

Understanding, Lucas listened carefully.

There was no sound at all.

"The nurse said basement laboratory," Lucas murmured. "Do you think she meant literally or figuratively?"

Tristan looked up the stairs leading towards the second floor. They both moved their heads, the motion almost simultaneous as they continually scanned their surroundings, listening intently. Tristan stalked out along the hall leading farther back into the house.

"We don't have back up," Tristan spoke equally softly. "It would suck to have him ambush us from behind. We do this by the book, together. Clear and sweep each room in sequential order, top to bottom."

Lucas sucked in a deep breath, his nerves on edge. Adrenaline spiked through his body as they silently climbed upwards, guns drawn. They paused once again to listen carefully at the top of the stairs. Lucas could clearly see the three bedrooms and tiny bathroom that filled the first floor.

With silent gestures Tristan indicated he'd take the two on the right-hand side, Lucas was to take the left. Grateful for the carpet that masked their footsteps, Lucas swung left and carefully walked to the open bedroom door. In quick, crisp moves he pressed his back against the wall, swinging into the room gun first.

He briefly scanned across the empty room, taking in all the hidey-holes a person could fit within. Lucas strode quickly into the area and walked clockwise around it, pushing back curtains, opening the closet and checking under the bed.

Satisfied Harper wasn't present, Lucas left. Repeating the process for the tiny bathroom Lucas checked the area carefully. Not finding anything, he then went to meet Tristan back in the hallway. He indicated with a jerk of his head that they should go back downstairs. The two men silently went back to the ground floor.

Feeling on edge, Lucas trailed Tristan from room to room, sequentially checking every square inch of the house. As if by mutual agreement they left the kitchen—and its doorway down into the cellar—until last. Lucas glanced at his watch when they entered their final room and noticed it had taken them less than five minutes to clear the house.

It felt like an eternity. Impatience knotted his gut and a fine sheen of sweat coated his back. Electric energy hummed through his body and Lucas knew his senses had heightened the farther they'd progressed. They were now razor sharp. Attempting to calm his skyrocketing heart rate he breathed deeply, calmly. It didn't quell the jitters of his excitement. He knew this last step was the most crucial. Either they'd find Harper or not—but as always before he crashed through an unknown door,

Lucas knew the next few minutes could be his last. It had always affected him deeply, but now he'd found Abigail he realised he had something to come back in one piece for.

It felt wonderful but terrifying at the same time. His actions had always been his own, the only influence he'd worried about was how he'd felt. With shock he understood now he cared about Abigail and how his actions would influence her, how she would react to something he chose to do.

He froze when he discovered he didn't just care about Abigail, he also loved her deeply.

Knowing he would need to think more upon this epiphany later, Lucas put it away and focused on the task at hand. When Lucas had paused Tristan had also, silently querying what had stopped him. Lucas shook his head and signalled with a thumbs up that he was fine. They continued to the doorway leading into the basement.

It stood open, but no sound issued from the lower level. Slower now, inching their way down the stairs, Lucas found his mind full of questions, computing everything at an enormously fast pace. He wondered if this was a setup, if perhaps the nurse had called Harper to inform him that he would be having visitors soon and the doctor waited below ready to ambush them and blow them away the instant they showed their faces.

Or perhaps Harper was long gone, all their caution and checks useless and for nothing. Lucas closed his thoughts off when he almost began to worry how drawing this search out over days or weeks might affect Abby. Again, he couldn't think like that, he needed to remain focused.

Never had his attention been so easily diverted by anyone, let alone a woman. His focus had always been on the mission at hand. It felt unusual to have his focus split, his mind distracted all the time by thoughts of Abigail.

Tristan moved, fluidly pressing his back against the wall on the third last step. Immediately Lucas mimicked his motion, his brain snapping back into the game.

"You ready?" Tristan murmured softly.

Nodding, Lucas clung to the image of Abigail, then packed it away to the darkest corner of his brain. He wouldn't be able to do this with his attention split, and he needed to learn how to love his woman but still keep her out of his conscious mind while he worked. Tristan's life – and just as importantly, Lucas' own life – depended on it.

Taking a steadying breath, Lucas met his partner's eyes. Tristan searched his gaze for a moment, seeming to find whatever he looked for. He nodded and indicated Lucas should move out five feet to the other side when they entered, that Tristan would take the right-hand side in the sweep.

After conveying this message, Tristan lowered his hand.

Lucas made a circle with his thumb and forefinger in the classic 'okay' sign to show he understood and accepted his partner's suggestion. Tristan nodded, then lifted up three fingers, counted down to two, then one – and quick as a blink, one directly after the other, they raced down the remaining stairs and into the basement.

Gun held steady, Lucas scanned the room in one smooth, brief motion. Part of his brain assimilated the fact a man sat at a long bench in a stained white coat, seeming engrossed in whatever he was doing. Knowing from past experience that an easily spotted focus could prove to be a decoy, he continued his search. Exclusive focus on a single target often resulted in missing other, hidden, problems. The simple, understandable mistake could prove deadly. Lucas made a complete visual sweep of the basement, taking it all in for a few seconds. The bulk of the space was filled up by a large, long wooden bench. Beakers and glass bottles were lined up side by side. A small laboratory grade oven sat over in one corner with a metal cabinet next to it, covered by a lot of hazard stickers warning of explosive danger, fire hazards and biochemical threats encased within.

The room had been converted into a small, but perfectly professional, working laboratory to Lucas' untrained eye. He didn't linger over his assessment, doing as he was trained to, glancing over everything quickly and returning his attention and weapon back on the man.

"Paul Harper, let's see your hands," Tristan called out in a commanding, firm tone.

Harper looked up from his work. He held his hand steady, the pipette he used still aloft. He wore a white laboratory coat over a blue oxford shirt, the top few buttons undone. Harper's dark hair was heavily salted with iron grey, and he had a neatly trimmed beard that showed almost completely white with age.

Lucas' gaze registered that beneath the shirt, however, was an athletic man only barely past his prime. Should Harper choose to make this difficult he would not be an easy target to physically subdue. Lucas bet himself silently ten pounds the doctor still regularly worked out, even though he had to be in his early sixties.

"Drop it," Lucas cautioned Harper, both he and Tristan in a classic fighting stance, neither of their weapons wavering for an instant.

"What do you think you're doing?" Harper insisted indignantly. "I am in the middle of some critical experiments here. You idiots can't just come barging in here and—"

"Lower the pipette slowly, Dr Harper," Tristan backed him up in a tone that brooked no argument. "And keep your hands visible to us, or else I will come over there and make you lower them."

"Don't shoot!" Harper shouted, his voice high and shrill. "My work is critical for—"

"I said now, Doctor," Tristan insisted.

Lucas took a step forward menacingly and Tristan followed.

Harper scooted from his chair and knelt behind the bench, hidden now all except for the top of his head.

"Stand up, Harper!" Lucas shouted, coming forward another step, his gun raised and ready to shoot. "Harper!"

Paul Harper half stood then, lifting the large barrels of a shotgun up and resting his elbows onto the smoothly polished wood of the large bench.

"Fuck!" Lucas swore.

Both he and Tristan dived for cover as an enormous explosion rent through the room. Glass shattered and particles went flying, shrapnel cutting through the air as the boom echoed for a few seconds. Both Lucas and Tristan were almost prone on the floor, covering their heads for protection. Lucas looked wildly behind him and noticed a large chunk of the concrete wall had been blown out by the shell.

If either he or Tristan caught one of those bullets they'd lose a limb—or far worse.

Lucas knelt on the cool slab of the basement floor to give himself some height and held his gun in a double-handed grip for extra support. He squeezed off two quick shots at the doctor, forcing him to cower back behind the bench before Tristan yelled at him.

"Sloan, no! These solvents are flammable."

Lucas paused and frowned.

"We can't leave," he insisted.

"Don't shoot him, you'll blow the place up!" Tristan snapped. "Think of something else."

Tristan turned and crawled around the edge of the laboratory wall. Lucas strained his neck to follow the path his partner had taken, worried Tristan might be putting himself at risk so Lucas could do something insane to take out Harper, like rush him.

It only took a moment, but Lucas realised both the bench and the steep angle downward that Harper would have to aim the shotgun would be enough cover to protect Tristan's body from Harper's range.

Lucas internally debated the chances of a stray bullet really causing an explosion or not. He sniffed the air and could smell the acrid bitterness of evaporating solvent. Maybe Tristan was right. But honestly, what was he supposed to do to subdue Harper? Use his iron will? Bribe him? Use harsh language?

Harper took their distraction to his own advantage and squeezed off another round from the shotgun. The explosion came far too close to Lucas' head for his comfort, concrete dust and small pellets raining down on him from the new hole in the wall.

"What the fuck am I supposed to do?" Lucas yelled back to Tristan, incensed. "Training didn't exactly cover this!"

Lucas crawled on his belly towards the centre of the room, hoping that by keeping low it would force Harper either to stand up fully and give Tristan a clear shot at him, or just dissuade Harper from shooting at him altogether.

"Come on out and fight me. You wanted me badly enough to break into my home, to threaten me and try to carry me off to prison," Harper screamed, clearly pushed beyond some inner limit.

Lucas could no longer see Tristan or work out what he planned, and decided the entire situation had already gone to hell. He, for one, was willing to risk shooting the bastard and hope for the best. Heaven knew Harper was all too trigger-happy right now. Lucas decided he had to shoot, his only other option was to do nothing and risk sooner or later Harper blasting a shotgun pellet sized hole in him.

Comparatively speaking, Lucas' small weapon should not be as destructive, or as likely to set off an explosion. Neither did he have the least desire to stop a round from that shotgun. Using his own weapon would be the lesser evil, he figured.

Ducking his head around the corner of the bench, Lucas saw Harper crouched. The doctor still leaned on the thick wood, shotgun swerving madly as he sought a clear shot. Glass beakers and bottles had been knocked all over, some of them broken on the ground, some merely tumbled around the bench. Lucas squatted, hunched on the back of his heels so he could pivot around the corner but move back just as quickly should Harper shoot at him again.

"Give it up, Harper!" Lucas shouted, hoping beyond everything Tristan would use the opportunity to do something. "I've had enough of this shit. Put the shotgun down and I won't bloody well shoot you."

Harper swivelled his head around and stared wildly at Lucas. Lucas held his gun steady, leaning back ready, at Harper's slightest twitch, to duck again for cover behind the safety of the bench. Harper's arms shook and Lucas raised his gun to aim at the man's chest.

"Just put the gun down," Lucas spoke calmly, though his heart thundered so loudly it nearly deafened him. He scrambled mentally to continue talking, to keep Harper's attention on him so Tristan could do whatever he could.

"We can talk about this outside, or down at the office. No one needs to get hurt. Just think about this."

In the space of a single heartbeat Lucas saw Tristan come up behind Harper. His partner had turned his gun around, clearly intending to use the butt end to take Harper out without having to discharge his weapon. Harper seemed to almost sense him.

The elderly man whirled backwards, catching Tristan in the jaw with the base of the shotgun. Blood gushed from somewhere on or near Tristan's face— Lucas couldn't see exactly where as Tristan immediately dropped like a stone to the floor.

Lucas sprang up to protect his partner, placing his body between where Tristan had fallen and where Harper stood.

Lucas shot Harper in the thigh and reached out with his other hand to grapple for the shotgun. Harper collapsed against the bench, roaring with the pain. Blood sprang from the bullet wound. Lucas wrenched the shotgun out of Harper's grip and threw it as far across the room as he could manage.

"You can't steal my work! I've spent decades of my life on this. I won't let you ruin me like this." Harper screamed.

Satisfied he now wouldn't be hit in the back by Harper, Lucas stumbled to where Tristan had fallen. He was relieved to see that the blood that trickled down his face was from a nasty gash at the side of his mouth, not some deeper, more dangerous head wound that would need immediate attention. Lucas sagged, glad. Tristan hadn't suffered a broken nose or something more devastating.

Whoosh.

A harsh shout of laughter echoed around the concrete room. Lucas turned, his gun raised again as he fully expected Harper to have pulled another weapon out from who knew where. Harper brandished an automatic lighter.

"What the fuck?" Lucas gasped.

A flash of searing heat ignited before his very eyes. Most of the broken bottles of spilled solvents lit up instantly, the overpowering smell of burning chemicals hitting Lucas like a physical blow. The papers scattered across the bench quickly smoked and caught fire, fuelling the flames further.

Tristan groaned as he held his head and struggled to find his feet.

"Mate, get up," Lucas ordered urgently as he stepped forward carefully, trying to get a tight grip on Harper.

Harper fought him furiously. For a man twice Lucas' age he had a lot of strength and determination on his side.

Harper landed a solid blow on Lucas' jaw. Lucas grunted and saw dots cross his vision as he let Harper go and closed his eyes. Forcing himself through the pain Lucas sucked in a deep breath, opened his eyes again and continued to grapple with the older man. Almost appearing as if he enjoyed himself Harper didn't let up, still punching out at him. Lucas dodged a few of the swings, but again was caught unawares as a second blow landed.

This time Lucas stumbled back, dazed but not out of the fight yet.

Harper took the opportunity to feed his notebook into the flames, throwing more of his paperwork into the fire and feeding its voracious appetite. Lucas wondered if Harper had simply given up hope, or whether he was being savvy and tried to get rid of the evidence they could have used against him.

Lucas tried to snatch some of the papers away, but Harper splashed solvent onto Lucas' arm. He could feel the searing heat of the fire and took a step back. He didn't really know what kind of evidence might be in the papers Harper burnt, but Lucas wasn't willing to turn into a human fireball to try to find out.

"Harper, let it go. We have to leave before this whole place goes up in flames," Lucas insisted, coughing as the chemicals entered his lungs.

Harper shouted, "No—" and seemed about to say more, but instead began wheezing. Thick smoke rose to the ceiling, clouds of it rolled across the concrete. Lucas wondered if the kitchen above them had floorboards or some insulation that might act as temporary protection.

The small room quickly began to fill not only with smoke, but also with fumes from the solvents. Lucas noticed Harper's jeans were soaked dark with blood. He knew he couldn't have hit an artery—Harper would have been unconscious if not dead by now if he had—but the man would need medical attention in minutes or else he could die.

"Harper, let's go, you need help. Tristan, get the fuck up."

Tristan groaned, clearly not quite with it yet. Harper continued to throw papers into the fire. Lucas made a split-second decision, choosing to crouch beside his partner and pull him into a half-seated position. Harper was hampered by the shot in his leg, but should he have chosen he would have been perfectly capable of hobbling across the room and up the stairs. At that moment, Tristan didn't seem conscious of anything except for a splitting jaw ache and a seriously throbbing head.

Hauling an arm under his shoulder and grunting with the exertion, Lucas got Tristan unsteadily to his feet, almost fully supporting his friend's weight as Tristan got his bearings.

Smoke continued to fill the room as the fire spread, glass bottles exploding around them. Tristan coughed. Lucas propelled him towards the stairs, pushing him gently to urge him to leave first.

"I'll get Harper. Go!" Lucas insisted.

Either too dazed or confused to argue, Tristan staggered, clinging to the banister when he made it. Lucas crouched down on his haunches to avoid the worst of the fumes and crossed back into the room to find Harper.

Raising his hands to protect his face from the rapidly growing flames, Lucas was astonished to see Harper busily feeding the fire not only with papers but also test tubes that appeared to be full of blood and glass bottles filled with clear fluids and solvents.

The air reeked of a mixture of scents, formaldehyde and ethanol the most pungent of them. With another *whoosh* the bench truly caught fire, the blaze now running along its length and nearly spanning the width of the whole laboratory.

Harper seemed completely unconcerned by the steadily growing inferno, almost appearing caught up in his own crazy world. Lucas struggled to see a way for him to cross the fire and get to Harper.

He honestly didn't think he would be able to, and the solvent still clinging to his shirt worried him. Lucas didn't relish jumping and his clothes igniting, or being seriously burned. He wasn't certain there was enough open room for him to make it. The fire grew at an astonishing speed and grew before his eyes.

More importantly, Lucas didn't trust that he wouldn't catch alight if he did something as stupid as leap through the flames.

"Harper!" Lucas shouted, coughing as he inhaled a lungful of the grit now filling the air. "Har—" he couldn't even finish the second time, choking so bad he bent over double, wheezing to catch his breath.

Closing his eyes to stop the small particles from the smoke wafting in the air from scorching him, Lucas heard more glass exploding and the undeniable roar of the fire growing in strength and intensity. Thick, black plumes of smoke now belched from the blaze. The top of the basement and stairs were steadily smothering the room, making it increasingly impossible to see a thing.

"Sloan, forget it," Tristan called over the sound of the blaze.

The crackles and pop of the flames devouring wood increased in tempo, the fire licking hungrily at everything in its path. Harper's chuckles had weakened and when Lucas strained his eyes to see the elderly man he couldn't spot him, though whether Harper had fallen to the floor or was beyond the thick fog Lucas couldn't tell.

"Sloan!" Tristan called from the staircase.

Lucas crouched and made his way back to the stairs, the heat prickling his skin even through his clothes.

"Sloan! Come on, let's go!" Tristan screamed from the top of the stairs.

Lucas made it to the base of the staircase. As he reached out to touch the banister he swore and pulled his hand back in a rush. The wood burnt him. Running up the stairs, sweating from the heat and his eyes tearing up from the sting of the smoke, he huffed a laugh when he saw Tristan.

Wobbling he looked like he'd been in a pub brawl. One side of his face already was darkly discoloured, bruised and swollen, the dried blood caking over his skin to form a crust that began at the corner of his mouth. Soot stained his face and he rubbed his neck, clearly stiff and sore.

"You must be getting old," Lucas said with a laugh.

They hurried through the kitchen.

"You don't look like you've been relaxing at a picnic yourself, Sloan," Tristan retorted. "You're covered in soot and look like a scrawny chimney boy."

"Yeah, well at least I don't look like I was the loser of a Friday night tiff down at the local pub, mate," Lucas slung back with a laugh that ended in a cough.

A small explosion rocked the house, the floor moving beneath Lucas' feet as something blew up in the basement. Lucas and Tristan exchanged glances and ran for the front door.

"Do you think he can make it out?" Lucas huffed. He ripped open the back door.

"No chance," Tristan insisted as they raced across the back lawn and into the garden next door.

A siren wailed in the distance.

They both ducked down as another small explosion sounded and smoke poured out of the back windows of Dr Harper's house. Lucas noticed quite a number of people had come out onto the street and instinctively he took a few steps in that direction, wanting to see.

Tristan grabbed him by the arm.

"You look exactly like you've been in that fire, mate," Tristan reminded him. "Might not be a good idea to go and watch with the crowd."

"Ah, yeah." Lucas nodded.

They jogged through a half dozen gardens and came out onto the footpath well up the street, walking back to the car with their heads down but not so fast they would attract attention.

Lucas noticed both Kimber and Abigail standing beside their car, Kimber tapping her foot impatiently and Abigail with her arms crossed over her chest. Something deep inside Lucas eased when he saw her.

"There they are," Abigail said to Kimber as she spotted them.

Kimber raced towards them, but Abigail stood and waited.

Unable to help himself, Lucas turned around quickly and looked back down the street. Smoke poured from the house and the roof appeared as if it were steaming. Flames licked out along the cornices and small booms echoed up and down the street.

A small grin of satisfaction flickered at the corner of Lucas' mouth. He regretted the fact they hadn't been able to bring Dr Harper to justice, but he couldn't deny he felt some small amount of pleasure at the man's work being destroyed. The sound of sirens was noticeably closer as the two men hurried down the footpath next to Abby and Kimber.

Lucas glanced up and down Abigail's slender form, making certain she was unharmed.

"I'll ride with Kimber, you drive Abby," Tristan spoke as he tossed the car keys.

Lucas caught them easily.

"Meet you back at the office?" Lucas suggested.

Tristan tenderly touched the bruise that was forming on his jaw.

"I want to drop Kimber off at her flat, and then I wouldn't mind a hot shower and taking care of this." He indicated his swollen wound. "The paperwork over this will be a nightmare. Let's meet back in a few hours. Will that be okay?"

"Sure, I can drop Abby off at her place and clean myself up as well."

Anything further Lucas might have added was cut off as a horn sounded, unmistakably from a fire engine.

"Shit, they're only a street or two away," Lucas cursed.

They ran to their respective vehicles. Lucas unlocked the passenger door for Abby before bolting around to slide into the driver's seat.

A moment later and they'd pulled away, barely managing to turn out of the street before a fire engine entered from the opposite end.

Lucas glanced to Abby, reaching out to take one of her hands in his.

"You all right, darling?" he checked.

"I'm just glad you're back in one piece," she replied before she pressed a kiss to the palm of his hand.

He stroked her hair tenderly but needed to focus on the road.

"We're both exhausted, let's get to my place first," Abigail replied, seeming to read his frustration at not being able to act as he wished just now.

"Direct me, love, and I will follow," Lucas said.

Abby chuckled as they wound their way through the streets.

Chapter Seven

Lucas followed Abigail up a cracked footpath to a small flat. Bunches of flowers grew haphazardly in clumps, giving the area a homey feel. She opened the door with her key, entering the flat with an evident sigh of relief to be home.

He entered the warm dwelling, the place filled with pictures and furniture, the room cramped but not overwhelmingly so.

He paused on the threshold of the main living room, a little worried when Abby continued to the other side of the room before stopping and turning around. Lucas wanted to close the distance between them, but she'd been silent for the last ten minutes except for giving him directions.

A lot had gone on in the last few hours and Lucas wasn't sure what she thought of it all. He'd grown worried that she was truly upset she'd lost her chance for justice against Harper.

"Abby?" he queried, his heart in his throat.

"Did you set the fire on purpose?" she asked.

Surprised at the question, he shook his head.

"No, darling, Harper set it. He was mad as a hatter. Seemed to think we'd try to steal his work. Or, that was the impression I got as he threw his notes and research into a steadily growing solvent fire. He had a shotgun too. Tristan and I tried to bring him in, but in the end it was beyond us. I swear."

"I know you did your best," she answered in a timid voice. "I never doubted that of you."

Lucas watched while she listlessly plucked at the fabric on one of her couches. He waited, knowing there would be more but not sure exactly what she was getting at. With the air of telling him a great secret she worked up to voicing the words he could see all but bubbling out of her.

"I'd have been tempted to burn it all down myself," she confessed. "Is he still in there?"

Lucas nodded, though it took him a second to find the right words.

"He got caught in the laboratory. There was no way he could have escaped. I'm so sorry I can't bring him to justice, like I know I promised you. I swear I tried, though. I went back in for him after I got Tristan to the stairs, but the smoke was too thick and—" He didn't get to finish his rushed explanation. Abby had crossed the room back to him and flung herself at him. Only his quick reactions allowed him to open his arms in time to wrap them around her slender form.

She clung to him in a manner Lucas could easily get used to, the long tendrils of her soft hair smelling sweet against the stink of smoke in his nostrils. Lucas buried his head in the locks and inhaled her deeply, filling himself with her sweet scent. She squeezed him tightly, her words muffled against his clothes.

"I don't care in the least about justice, you gave me vengeance instead. I didn't wish for his death, and I'm not happy for it, but there's a balance there, for those other poor people whose deaths he caused. I'd have never wanted you to go back into flames of any sort for him, and certainly not because you'd think I'd want it. I don't ever want you to head into danger for me, okay?"

Lucas held her close.

"But you wanted answers, and I wanted to give them to you."

"Morrison called and said my blood work was fine," she explained.

Lucas sighed with relief.

"I'm glad to just put this behind me, to close the door and start a new chapter. Hopefully with you," she added shyly.

Lucas laughed and cupped her face, tilting her head up to his so he could bend down and plant a long, slow, searching kiss to her lips.

They kissed hungrily, each holding the other as if they would never let go. The kiss deepened and Lucas felt a hunger stir low within him. Something he knew could never thoroughly be assuaged. He moved his hands lower to cup Abby's round, pert arse.

He lifted her against him, pressing the heat of her crotch into his rapidly growing erection.

Abby's small hands were hot on him as she threaded her fingers through his hair. Long red strands fell around him in a curtain as her locks closed them in their own little world.

"I struggled to not think of you every moment while I was in there," he murmured huskily. "Even your memory distracted me madly. I realised in there I could no longer separate you from my every waking thought. I've fallen in love with you, Abigail Turner."

"I think I loved you from the moment you rescued me in my dream," she confessed in return, her voice a low whisper. "You were my hero then just as you are now. Your armour might be rusted in places, but you're still a knight, the pure silver of your honour shining through."

"I have never felt like some conquering hero or brave knight before. I have to be honest, though, when it comes to being your knight the thought appeals immensely. I'll do my best to never let you down, Abby," he promised.

The warmth of her smile, the light in those gorgeous eyes and the softness of her face drew him as no one ever had before. He couldn't believe he'd become so lucky to catch a woman like her. Lucas didn't ever want to take her for granted or see her hurt like she had been.

"If you hold me like this forever and ever then I doubt you could disappoint me, Lucas. I'd love to stay like this, always."

"I couldn't bear it if I didn't have you to return to," he whispered.

She sealed their lips together in a devastating kiss and pulled their bodies flush. He ached to be inside her, filling her in every way but at the same time he wanted to do it right.

"Where's your bedroom, darling?" he asked between searing hot kisses. "I want to do justice to you, want to—"

"I don't need any of that," she murmured before suckling on his lower lip.

Lucas groaned as heat shot through his belly and his erection pressed uncomfortably hard against his slacks.

"I just need you," she insisted. "Only you."

Lucas lifted her legs up, wrapping them around his waist as he looked around with one eye cracked open. The couch was right there and truth be told he didn't know if they'd make it to her bed.

He lowered her down slowly, loving the feel of her in his embrace. Lucas pushed Abby back into the soft cushions. They tore each other's clothes off. In seconds they were both naked—her knickers had been torn and his boxers had lost all three buttons. Lucas couldn't have cared less, as long, smooth expanses of Abigail's skin now lay open before him, calling for him to taste her.

Flicking his tongue out along her slender limbs, he tasted her, loving the way she tugged her fingers at his hair in her impatience.

"Fuck me," she pleaded, sending his blood pressure through the roof. "Right now, hard and hot. Please, Lucas, just fuck me right now."

A part of his brain reminded him about the condom. He swore and patted the ground around them, looking for his pants and that bloody piece of foil. Abigail groaned in frustration until she must have realised what he sought.

"No, no," she insisted, "we don't need that, I swear."

Lucas turned his attention fully back to her.

"I get tested regularly," he muttered, but any further comments were lost as their lips locked hungrily together once again. He knew in his heart they were beyond petty deceptions. The details could be worked out later, right now only their mutual need mattered.

So many small things could be fixed in the coming hours, his reports, her discussing options or any needs she'd have with Kimber, or perhaps Dr Morrison. Right now Lucas knew without a doubt the craving he felt in his blood for this woman superseded everything else.

"Tell me again," he purred, needing and wanting more than anything to hear her say the words.

Her green eyes burned hungrily into him. She lay back on the couch, her wild hair a mess around her face, framing her delicate features. She was easily the most beautiful person he had ever seen. Her lips were plump and red from the heat of their passion.

Like the most wicked and tempting of sirens she drew the moment out, before cupping his face in her hand and drawing him up so closely together their breaths mingled.

"I love you, Lucas Sloan," she whispered seductively, the most erotic words anyone had ever spoken to him. "You're my hero, my lover and my soul mate. I love you more than you could possibly ever know."

Lucas kissed her, tracing his fingers over her soft skin, stroking over the places he was learning to be her most sensitive, enticing sweet spots. He let one hand trail down to between her legs, gathering the moisture already pooled amongst her lips as he traced his thumb over the erect nub of her clit. Over and over he circled around that hard peak, enjoying the way it made her breaths come faster, her hips canting up to meet his every stroke. He could feel her heart beating harder against the wall of her chest, a pale pink flush of arousal staining her perfect, pale skin.

And still they kissed each other with a passionate, drugged intensity. He suckled her tongue, drawing it into his mouth and toying with it as he played with her body. Abigail turned out to be full of surprises. She took him in her hand, the heat of his erection straining as she stroked him firmly, up and down, nearly making him lose his mind with lust.

"Now, now, now," she pleaded with him, and he could no longer hold himself back.

He positioned his cock at the slick heat of her entrance.

"I love you, Abigail Turner," he said, wanting her to feel the truth and intensity behind his every word. "I love you with everything I have within me. You're my lover, my soul mate and the most perfect woman I have ever known. I want to be with you forever."

"Yes," she gasped, clawing at his hips to draw him inside her.

Giving her everything he could, he thrust deeply within her, all the way until his cock was fully sheathed and his balls bumped against the tender skin of her arse. Joined fully, as intimately as it was possible for a man and woman to be, he thrust into her, whispering promises of all the future would hold for them. She lifted her face and they kissed. Whether it was one long kiss or a series of hundreds he couldn't tell and didn't care.

As he rocked into her over and over he felt the climax between them grow and expand. Panting for breath, his back glistening with sweat, he plunged within her depths, thrusting harder with each stroke.

Abigail's head fell back, her hair streaming around her and over his arms as he cradled her to him. Her back arched and her body rippled around him, contractions shuddering hard through her. She screamed her release. Her pussy clenched his shaft, triggering his own peak. He pulsed into her, shooting his seed deeply, filling her with all his essence.

They shuddered together in pleasure, the whole of his focus, his senses and his life rooted only to her. She fell back against the couch, drained, exhausted. Lucas collapsed next to her, both of them panting hard and struggling to catch their breath.

He knew they would soon have to move. To bathe, maybe to nap briefly before they returned to the office and began the slow process of cleaning up the mess. But none of that bothered him, not any of it at all.

They had each other, nothing else mattered.

Lucas stretched out on the couch, cuddling Abigail close to him as they lazily shared the heat of their bodies with each other. He kissed her swollen lips. She stared at him, her eyes shining with happiness and love. Lucas couldn't believe how much he enjoyed seeing that light in her gaze. Already he could see the difference freedom and health returned to this woman. She was far stronger than she gave herself credit for. Lucas couldn't wait to learn more about her.

As they held one another, he traced his fingers tenderly over her soft skin. He drew random patterns as a world of possibilities opened up before him. He knew without a doubt they would spend their lives together, and he looked forward to seeing all the different facets of Abigail. In the few short days they'd known each other he'd already seen so much of her, he couldn't wait for them to surprise each other more over the coming months and years.

He kissed her again. It felt like a benediction, a blessing to start their new life, together for always. Lucas lifted his hand, stroked a tendril of hair away from her face and tucked it behind her ear. He cupped her jaw and he stared happily at her, completely at peace.

"I love you," she whispered.

Lucas smiled, his world utterly complete.

"I love you too, darling," he answered. Nothing in him questioned that it would be the first time of many he returned those words to her.

About the Author

Elizabeth Lapthorne has been writing professionally since 2002. She has a number of books released and is continually surprised by how much fun she has starting a new book and discovering new characters and situations that they put themselves in. She enjoys going to the gym (usually to chew over her latest problem scene), is rarely without a partially read book and has a weakness for chocolate.

Elizabeth Lapthorne loves to hear from readers. You can find her contact information, website details and author profile page at http://www.total-e-bound.com.

Total-E-Bound Publishing

www.total-e-bound.com

Take a look at our exciting range of literagasmic™
erotic romance titles and discover pure quality
at Total-E-Bound.